GW00832887

A Feast at Midnight

Justin Hardy & Yoshi Nishio

VIKING

VIKING

Published by the Penguin Group
Penguin Books Ltd, 27 Wrights Lane, London w8 5tz, England
Penguin Books USA Inc., 375 Hudson Street, New York, New York 10014, USA
Penguin Books Australia Ltd, Ringwood, Victoria, Australia
Penguin Books Canada Ltd, 10 Alcorn Avenue, Toronto, Ontario, Canada m4v 3b2
Penguin Books (NZ) Ltd, 182–190 Wairau Road, Auckland 10, New Zealand

Penguin Books Ltd, Registered Offices: Harmondsworth, Middlesex, England

First published 1995
1 3 5 7 9 10 8 6 4 2
First edition

Copyright © Justin Hardy and Yoshi Nishio, 1995
The moral rights of the authors have been asserted

All rights reserved.
Without limiting the rights under copyright
reserved above, no part of this publication may be
reproduced, stored in or introduced into a retrieval system,
or transmitted, in any form or by any means (electronic, mechanical,
photocopying, recording or otherwise), without the prior
written permission of both the copyright owner
and the above publisher of this book

Typeset by Datix International Limited, Bungay, Suffolk
Filmset in 11/14pt Baskerville Monophoto

Printed in Great Britain by Clays Ltd, St Ives plc

A CIP catalogue record for this book is available from the British Library

ISBN 0-670-86327-0

Contents

Master Glove

'My dear boy, a day in Paris without a pastry is a day not worth living.' Monsieur Vaudron's impersonation of an English gentleman left a little to be desired, but the platter of heavenly marquises au chocolat that he proffered was impossible to fault.

'No, thank you,' Magnus replied, somewhat surprised by the general heartiness of the appetites at this solemn occasion, 'I'm not hungry.'

Every conversation stopped in mid-sentence, and a madeleine plopped noisily on the carpet. Magnus had never been known to refuse food before, let alone a pastry with chocolate involved. Nor, more to the point, had his father, for it was his memory they were all gathered to honour. Magnus, not yet nineteen years old. The others, of all ages, were Father's comrades from the market: jolly Madame Partouche, the chocolatière, timid Tartouffe the baker, ruddy Robuchon the butcher, Pettit the fruiterer, and so many others whose names Magnus couldn't remember. And, of course, round Monsieur Vaudron, patron of the pâtisserie. Gourmets all, they had closed the market for the day and swapped the bright colours of their stalls for the dark suits of respect.

They had brought with them offerings they knew to have been Father's favourites. From where

Magnus stood in the tall doorway, it was quite a celebration of life, a harvest festival of thanks.

Magnus took a marquise from the outstretched plate, and the assembled guests heaved great sighs of relief, drawing him into the bosom of their company. For now that the old man had gone, they were the only family Magnus had left. Seeing them gathered now, he couldn't help but think back to the day he met them all for the very first time.

Magnus would never forget that birthday.

*   *   *

It was still dark outside when he was roused from sleep by the beam of a torch gliding across his face.

'Magnus . . .' came the soft voice from the darkness.

'Mmm,' was all Magnus could manage, as he pulled the covers over his head.

'Time to get up.' The gentle command was accompanied by a prod. Magnus poked his head out to find his father fully dressed in his outdoor clothes, his eyes smiling with boyish excitement. He clearly meant business.

'Why?'

'Because when a chap reaches double figures, society expects to see him marketing.'

'Marketing? Can I really?'

The old man nodded, and Magnus needed no more encouragement. He bounded out of bed, pulled on his baggy little sweater and flip-flopped down the passageway on the backs of his favourite red Converse All-Stars. Father waited patiently by the front door, immaculately casual as always, and offered Magnus his bomber jacket.

'Your shoes are supposed to go on you, not you on your shoes.'

'Yes, Papa.'

Ready to go, the two of them, old man and young boy, stood side by side in front of the hall mirror. Satisfied that they were now presentable, Father gave a gruff nod of approval and reached for the final touch to his shopping ritual, a ritual Magnus had watched so many times before from behind the banisters, but had never been allowed to share. He never knew exactly where Father went for all those hours, just that he always returned with an air of contentment, his tattered string bag full of delicious-smelling goodies. Now on went Father's floppy felt hat, and the picture was complete.

The heavy old door creaked open on to a whole new world for Magnus. As the two of them, hand in hand in the breaking light, made their way down the deserted grand avenues and up the narrow cobbled streets of Paris, neither one of them needed to talk. Their destination was the only place to be when you weren't actually eating: a place where grown-ups went to play. This was Magnus's first invitation to that moveable feast, the Parisian street markets. He was a grown-up now. He was ten years old.

Before they reached the top of the hill next to Sacré Coeur Magnus heard the rattle of ancient wooden carts on the cobbles and the symphony of booming voices and shrill cries from the assembled crowds. And suddenly, there before him was a bustling street teeming with movement and colour. Unstoppable old dames in their dusty slippers weaved between the mosaic of vegetable greens and pale yellows, accented by sunbursts of rosy tomatoes and Martinique bananas. Chefs bartered in the early spring light, pinching herbs and sniffing wild strawberries.

In amidst the throng, Magnus watched proudly as Father picked out the juiciest pears, still glistening with dew. The whole world seemed to know him, their friendly 'rosbif' gentilhomme, and they shook him by the hand and kissed him on both cheeks. To them the rather wobbly old man was that most reassuring of Englishmen. The 7th Baron Gove was a romantic of the old school, who had left London on the Grand Tour and never gone back. Resisting the advances of an England overrun by tasteless food and public-school bullies, he had lived in blissful exile all over Europe, settling finally in Paris. Following an impulsive marriage to a young French actress, the birth of a son and heir had provided him with a pleasure he had never expected. Sadly, the same could not be said for his wife, whose elevation to an English Lady entitled her to a life in the fast stream, a life she was determined to enjoy unencumbered by a child who merely reminded her of her passing youth. But for Magnus, the attentions of one adoring parent were quite enough to be going on with. There was warmth enough to be found in the deep pockets of Father's cardigan.

'This is my son,' beamed Father as the plump fishwives gathered round and clucked.

'He is a young chef, *non*? Like his father?' They chuckled, emitting great ripples of laughter from deep within their ample *poitrines*.

Magnus felt a surge of pride in the man who drew so many admiring smiles from the men and excited glances from the women. But, more than that, he felt himself rising to a challenge: to become, in their eyes, a gourmet worthy of his father. He would become the saucier's apprentice, and be welcomed into a secret society.

The market seemed to go on for ever. Exotic island fruits gave way to racks of plump geese, then to enormous wheels of cheese. And all the while, Father shuffled around, burrowing and prodding, fingers testing for the ingredients that would reach their peak at exactly the moment he wanted. His aquiline nose scoured for scents, his eyebrows dipped up and down to express approval. And each satisfactory find was passed down to Magnus for a second opinion: an opinion that grew in confidence at every stall. The string bag was soon bursting, and Father's floppy felt hat was now commissioned to take on its secondary, but critical, function: the holder of excess.

Father and son hadn't noticed their own hunger until they found themselves up against the window of the sweet-smelling pâtisserie in the rue du Poteau. The display inside was like a collection of finely crafted jewels: emerald and sapphire fruits glistening in their juices, carefully laid in settings of golden pastry. But nothing caught the eye quite like the plump, buttery madeleines and the little Chantilly-filled choux, under their blankets of dark chocolat amer.

'Feel up to a small birthday cake or two?' Father suggested, leading the way. Magnus's tummy leapt in anticipation.

'And it would be a shame to pass up Vaudron's pains au chocolat.'

By the time Father beckoned to the *garçon* with a conspiratorial nod of his head, Magnus's face was already covered in chocolate.

'Has the *patron* got any marquises ready yet?'

'*Pour vous? Bien sûr, monsieur.*'

'We don't want to spoil our appetite, so we'll share one. Oh, and another chocolat chaud for the lad, with just an inkling of Cointreau.' The *garçon*, in on the conspiracy, beetled away with a wry smile on his face. Magnus looked apprehensive.

'Something to wash it all down with. You know, Magnus . . .' the old man leaned forward, as if imparting a state secret '. . . a day in Paris without a pastry is a day not worth living. You, my dear boy, have inherited that famous Gove sweet tooth. Now tuck in. We've got a bit more to get through to build up our energy for some serious cooking.'

The gastronomic day had only just begun.

The kitchen in their apartment in the 14th *arrondissement* was quite unlike the other rooms. The clutter of tattered leather books and crumbling picture frames had no place in this inner sanctum. Its high walls boasted gleaming copper pans of every shape and size, while the spotless wooden chopping block was crowned with row upon row of glistening knives and pots of exotic herbs. It was a world that had seemed out of reach to Magnus until today, when Father allowed him to get up on a chair by the cutting-board and act as sous-chef. After years of sitting and watching, of tasting and keeping favourite recipes in a scrapbook, the time had finally come for one now so advanced in years to take part in the actual creation.

'Pear knife, please,' Father commanded. Magnus scoured the hanging armoury for a pear knife, whatever that might be.

'The little one, with the old wooden handle and the curved, serrated blade.' There were quite a few that fitted that description.

'The one Scoffier gave me at the Ritz in '34.' No closer.

'The one you used to use to cut out pictures for the scrapbook.' Ah, that one.

'Thank you.' With swift, expert movements, Father cut into the juicy flesh of the pears. As quickly as Father could discard pips and long, curly pieces of the skin on to the cutting-board, Magnus efficiently cleared them away.

'Today I have something really special in mind for us: Poire Belle Hélène, one of Scoffier's favourites. He named it after your grandmother.' Father took a ceramic dish from the freezer, and winked at Magnus as he pulled back the muslin to reveal the glace au vanille inside. Now I see, thought Magnus. That's what he was up to all yesterday afternoon.

'Why don't you give this a stir?' Over by the stove, Father had already started to melt dark chocolate in an antique double-boiler. Magnus was delighted to be given a task he had watched Father perform so many times. The double-boiler was his favourite contraption, and Magnus began to stir with a concentration worthy of a chess grand-master.

'She was one of the great beauties of her genera-tion, your grandmother, and when Scoffier came to London in the twenties he courted her with food. History doesn't relate whether he succeeded, but she talked about his desserts until the day she died. And he, in return, dedicated this sinful but sumptuous dish to her.' The perfect slivers of pear were now elegantly arranged on the ice-cream, and Magnus took great care to ladle the melted choco-late over it without messing up the delicate pattern.

Father did not believe in formality, so he had asked Marie-Claire to set out the silver on the rough oak table in the kitchen before she left on her day off. For Magnus, it was lovely and cosy to be sitting close together on the comfy chairs. Father lifted the silver dome with a grand flourish: 'Poire Beau Magnus.' Father did believe in presentation – tempt with the eye, he said, and the pleasure was doubled. Looking at the inviting pear sundae, Magnus had to agree.

Ten proud candles cast a glow on the two expect-ant faces. Magnus leant forward and took a really deep breath.

'Wait! You must make a wish first.'

Magnus held his breath and tried to think of something he really wanted. Not easy. He thought

8

very hard. He knew that what he really wanted was something he couldn't have: for his parents to get together again. He wanted to see them every night, both standing in the doorway of his bedroom as they switched out the light, then Father gently guiding his mother across the hall, his hand barely touching the small of her open-backed dress. But Magnus was old enough to know that there was no point in wishing for that. It was a waste of a wish to ask for something that was so far beyond his reach. The best wishes are those that can be helped along by our own willpower. Magnus, as he thought, looked into the smiling, wrinkled face of Father. He saw an old man who never complained, but tired more and more easily. Magnus wished Father would live for ever. That they would stay there in Paris and go marketing, and fill in their scrap-book, for ever – even when Magnus was as old as Father.

Magnus held the knife up and, to a great round of applause from Father, brought it down. He then politely offered up the first serving to the chef de cuisine.

From the apartments opposite it must have looked quite a sight: two boys stuffing themselves in a dimly lit kitchen, entirely absorbed in the matter at hand, oblivious to the nine million other Parisians dancing and arguing the night away. The old lady who lived across the way saw an old man standing up, contentedly patting his tummy as he came walking over to the window. But then his face stopped smiling. It started drowning, mouth wide

open, gasping for air. His whole body shook uncon-
trollably, his hands grabbing wildly first at his
throat, then at his chest, as he slid inelegantly down
out of sight.

'Papa? Papa? What's wrong?'

Father didn't answer. For the first time in
Magnus's life, there were no reassuring words. Just
the big old cardigan, crumpled on the floor, Father
inside it perfectly still, face contorted, eyes staring
out like one of the fish Magnus had seen in the
market.

The ambulance came quickly, called by the neigh-
bourly lady. Father had suffered a near-fatal heart
attack, and was to struggle through two more in
the hospital that night. He looked like a ghost when
Magnus was finally allowed to see him three days
later.

The hospital was the biggest place Magnus had
ever seen. There were more people there than even
at the market, and each one of the endless corridors
was bigger than their apartment. Old people and
sick people were everywhere, and Magnus couldn't
imagine anyone getting better in a place like that.

'Please come home, Papa.'

Father summoned a smile. 'Soon, my dear boy.
Very soon, I promise.'

'I don't want to be at home without you.'

'Now that's not a very polite thing to say to
Marie-Claire, is it?' At the doorway to his private
room Marie-Claire blinked away her tears.

'Sorry, Marie-Claire,' said Magnus, his head
bowed. Marie-Claire smiled for an instant, but

could not hold back her feelings any longer. She disappeared, her heels and the trumpet of her blowing nose receding urgently down the corridor.

'Come and sit here,' Father said, patting the space beside him on the starched white bedcover. 'We need to have a little chat, man to man.' Magnus nodded suspiciously and sat down.

'My dear boy, now that you are grown up, it is important for us to be candid with each other. I don't like this situation any more than you do, but we must both learn to make the best of it. The long and short of it is, I will have to stay here for a little while.'

'How long?' Magnus perked up. He knew Father wouldn't want to stay in a place like this for very long. He thought that he would make that chocolate charlotte recipe for when Father came back. That would be a good surprise.

'I don't know exactly, yet. But it does mean that I can't be at home to look after you.'

'I'll come and live here.' This wasn't as bad as he thought.

'No, Magnus, this place is for old people like me. You need to be with young people, make friends your own age.'

'But –'

'No, no. The decision has already been made. It's your mother's idea really, but I must say I can't disagree. It's probably for the best. You'll start at a school back in England. Very good, academically, and er . . . you know, beautiful countryside and all that . . .' Father trailed off. Seeing

Magnus's face drop to the hospital basement, he rallied once more. 'It's called Dryden Park. A preparatory school for young gentlemen, like yourself. It was my school actually, some time ago of course, but I do remember it very well . . .' He drifted off again. He really couldn't say that Dryden Park and its like were precisely the reason he had abandoned England in the first place.

'I'm sure it's even better now. Probably a bit like a hotel. No room service, but apparently they're very proud of their cuisine.' Father stopped dead. What else could be say? That he hated the idea of sending his son to the sort of place that had brought him nothing but misery? But things must surely be very different now. And anyway, what were the alternatives? There were none. The doctor had diagnosed blocked arteries, and his wife had of course immediately blamed it on his eating habits. Magnus would eat 'sensible' meals at boarding-school. According to her, boarding was back in fashion among the 'smart' set in London, and it was just the solution for Magnus.

Father was in no position to argue, lying in his hospital bed. He had fought hard to keep Magnus, with the promise of a stable home and a good education, which he had provided himself. Until now. But he couldn't bear to have Magnus watch him die. Better for him to remember his father as merely old, rather than infirm – or worse.

'It will only be for a while,' he lied. He held Magnus tightly, and let him cry.

*

The black London taxi threaded its way through the tiny single-track road crossing the vast moor. The drizzle had turned into a full gale about two hundred miles ago.

The usually uninterested sheep looked up, mildly bemused by the curious urban creature roaring its diesel engine so far from home. Inside, perched on the edge of the back seat, sat Magnus, not knowing that his sense of impending doom was a familiar feeling for all Dryden Park boys at they approached the school. The bleak landscape that rushed by the window was how Magnus had imagined the moon looked. Far from the vibrant colours of the rue du Poteau in the gloss of the spring sunshine, here was a grey-green scrubland covered in a dull coat of English summer sky.

The grim-faced taxi-driver was a far cry from his chatty counterparts who raced battered Citroëns round and round the place de la Concorde. He raced, instead, with the surly annoyance of a man who smells his tea getting cold on the kitchen table. Even the relentless clicking of the meter did nothing to ease his disgruntlement. Magnus could almost hear him wondering to himself how he was going to find a fare back to London all the way out here.

Magnus's first day in England was not going according to plan. Mother had not been at Heathrow to meet him as promised. Instead, there was just the grumpy driver standing there with a sign saying 'MASTER GLOVE'.

The Welcoming Committee

Just when Magnus thought they had been travelling so long that they were about to fall off the other end of this small island, a huge wrought-iron gateway loomed into view ahead of him. It was imposing not so much for its imperious size and forbidding black railings as for its singular, almost ghostly presence. Out here, beyond the moors and the forest, it just stood all alone. There was no gatehouse. The gate was clearly chained shut to keep people out. Little did Magnus know that its purpose was also to keep people in.

The taxi screeched to such an abrupt halt that Magnus was thrown forward against his trunk. Then he was tipped out into the country lane by the surly driver with no name, no voice and even less charm. He simply held out his sweaty hand while Magnus peeled away notes from the money Father had given him for emergencies. By the time Mr Surly was through, Magnus was in no position to buy his way out of any future problems. As the very last note disappeared into the bunched fist, quicker than a Formula One race car through a pit stop, the black cab was heading back to wherever it came from, leaving Magnus to face the gates and whatever lay beyond.

There was a sign. Although it was hardly visible

through the thick foliage, it was a sign nevertheless. Magnus could just make out the peeling lettering that told him where he was:

DRYDEN PARK

PREPARATORY SCHOOL FOR BOYS
AGED 7 TO 12

So he was in the right place. For a moment Magnus had clung to the optimistic notion that Mr Surly had also been Mr Goofy, and had dropped him off at the wrong place. He would have had to return home to Father, shrugging his shoulders, saying that he was terribly sorry, he had tried but he couldn't find this Dryden Park, and so maybe he should just stay in Paris after all. But here it was. Or at least here was the sign, and some gates with an endless drive beyond.

Magnus thought hard about what he could say to Father: 'Well, I went there, and it was very nice and everything, but there was no school. For starters, the gates were locked. I think they were probably full up already.' But he knew that this would not do. Not that Father would be angry. Just disappointed.

So Magnus shrugged and sighed. He bent down and lifted up one end of the trunk that now seemed

Father's
Poire Belle Hélène

(serves 4)

For the ice-cream:
200 ml double cream
200 ml single cream
1 small vanilla pod
50g icing sugar, sieved

For the dessert:
4 ripe diplomat pears
2 tsps caster sugar
150g dark chocolate
Poire William liqueur (optional)

If you want to use ready-made ice-cream, start this recipe at Number 6.

1 Set the freezer to the coldest setting. (If you are using an ice-cream maker, follow its directions with the above ingredients.)

2 Put the double and single creams and the vanilla in a saucepan and gently simmer over a low heat for a few minutes, being careful not to let it boil. Take off the heat and let it sit for 15 minutes. Remove the vanilla pod.

3 In a freezer-proof bowl, lightly whip the mixture until thick but not firm.

4 Gradually stir in the icing sugar. Allow to cool.

5 Cover and then place the cream in the freezer, stirring well every 20 minutes until completely frozen.

6 Skin and core the pears. Cut into slivers.

7 Immediately place the slivers in a saucepan and sprinkle with the caster sugar. Add enough water to cover all the fruit.

8 Simmer gently for 30 minutes or until the pears are softened.

9 Break the dark chocolate into small pieces and melt, preferably in a double-boiler, adding a hint of Poire William if you like.

10 Scoop the ice-cream into serving dishes, arrange the pears around the side and carefully ladle the chocolate on top.

Father's tip: If you do not have a double-boiler, melt the chocolate this way: fill a saucepan with three inches of water and simmer. Break the chocolate into pieces and put in a heatproof bowl that is a bit bigger than the saucepan. Put the bowl in the saucepan, so the water just touches the bottom. Stir the chocolate as it melts.

larger even than himself, and started to drag it across the gravel to the gateway. It reminded him of a château Father had taken him to in Alsace: great oak portals that had been locked up since its owner had lost his head two hundred years before.

And, sure enough, there was a big rusty padlock, and no way around or over the high stone walls that jutted out from either side of the iron gates. As an obstacle, this was becoming a genuine excuse. Except . . . Except that there was a very small gap where the gates didn't quite hang properly. Magnus stood for a moment and looked back at the countryside that lay between him and home, at the dark-green forest that would give way to the stubbly moor, then the rolling hills, the little villages, the messy suburbs, the factories, the city centre, the airport, and finally France. Magnus liked walking; he particularly enjoyed going through the Tuileries and along the Seine all the way to Île de la Cité, as he and Father always did on a Sunday afternoon. But England to Paris was going to be a bit too far, even for him. Best get on with the job at hand, Father would say, and Father knew best.

Magnus squeezed himself through the narrow gap and wrestled with his trunk. He wrenched it through the gates and dragged it along that endless drive under the overarching lime trees. All the comings and goings they must have seen. Magnus was sure they were winking at each other as he struggled along, and whispering like the old dames in the market. Beyond the trees he came to a majestic parkland, spotted with red deer, which looked up to observe this newcomer. Their soft brown eyes seemed to offer their condolences.

Suddenly they were in a panic, turning on their hind legs and bolting away. Magnus had heard what they heard too. A great crack still seemed to echo amongst the trees hundreds of metres away. It was like the sound of a smack but louder, more violent. Like a fish at market being slammed down on to the cutting-board. Whatever this noise was, it wasn't friendly, and Magnus dropped his trunk, looking around in alarm. The crack was followed by a whoosh, and that whoosh was getting louder, as if the air was parting for the onslaught of something. Then there, directly above Magnus, heading straight for him, sped a round, hard missile – a ball.

Magnus waved his arms around in self-defence but realized in the nick of time this was not enough. He hurled himself to the ground. The ball rushed past his ear, bounced off his trunk high into the limes and was gone.

From the other side of a hillock came a great roar of approval, and Magnus was confused. But, as he soon discovered, that is a state most people never recover from when it comes to England's most heartfelt pastime: cricket.

Out on the square, hidden from the dazed Magnus, two small figures dressed in white raced back and forth between the wickets, to the consternation of the little fielders hopping up and down, and to the joy of the crowd seated in deckchairs on the boundary. It was the quintessential English moment, and, to celebrate the fact, the blood-orange late afternoon sun bowled up out of the clouds to warm everyone's faces.

'That was a jolly good six, wasn't it, sir?' yelled a third-former above the applause, determined to win favour with a member of staff. But this particular member of staff was a long way away and did not appreciate being dragged out of his afternoon's reverie, deep in the latest issue of his favourite read, the *Economist*.

Unlike most headmasters, Mr J. M. Trumper B.A. (Hons.) hated cricket, but he knew that it was fundamental to tradition, it kept the boys out of the changing rooms and, above all, it impressed prospective parents. And this year had been a particularly good one, with young Bathurst adding numerous centuries to his already formidable tally. Chaps like that might bring in twenty new boys, and, as the Education section of his *Economist* pointed out, a headmaster needed every new bug he could lay his hands on if he was to swim safely through this recession. Not to mention the prevailing trend against boarding-schools in general, perpetrated by the pinko media.

'Was that Bathurst again? Well played, sir,' the Headmaster spluttered, slapping his tweed-suited thigh. He peered into the distance, watching the red leather ball disappear over the trees. 'Expect we've lost the ball again, though. That's another £4.95 down the drain.' Could have been £9 though, he consoled himself, if he hadn't made such a good deal with Jacques of London, the last time he was up in town.

Yes, Dryden Park was doing just fine, no small thanks to himself, thought the Headmaster. He beamed happily at his boys gathered around him, and, up above, that big old sun beamed right back. Indeed he felt so cheerful that he reached over and plucked one of the dainty sandwiches from the tea trolley, to complete the moment's pleasure.

But it was not to be. A huge hand cracked down upon his, and the sandwich was rudely removed before it reached his open mouth.

'What the —' he blurted.

'Really, Headmaster. Could you not wait until after the innings?' came the curt reply.

If there was one person who could reduce even the Headmaster to a naughty boy, it was the Head Matron, Miss Plunder, standing there in all her fullness and finery, rooted to the spot like a grand old oak tree in autumnal red.

He sulked. 'The way Bathurst's playing, we shall all miss high tea.' Gloomy thought, to miss the old trough. But then he cheered up. 'Still, impressive for the prospective parents. Pretty sure we got those Abu Dhabi twins this afternoon.' Sheikh Al-Shab-something-or-other and his wife had been torn between Dryden and Wakeley Court, but Bathurst's performance today had, the Headmaster was sure, tipped the balance in Dryden's favour. The twins were a bit thick, but then £18,000 a year for the cash flow was £18,000 a year for the cash flow. The school would clear a good four grand, and the Sheikh was keen for his boys to be able to play tennis year round. The Headmaster was sure he would 'help', if he was handled right. The Headmaster could already picture the plaque being unveiled at the opening ceremony for the new indoor courts.

The Headmaster raised himself from his shooting-stick and peered over the hillock. He could make out a little boy waving his arms around and falling to the ground.

'And I'm not sure that that's not another £9,000 a year coming up the drive now.'

'The drive is out of bounds at this time of day!'

'No, no, Miss Plunder. A new bug. Now what's his name? Umm, ummm.' He flipped through the pages of his *Economist*, and there it was, hastily scrawled at the top: Gove, M. – Heathrow, 3 p.m. 'We'd better muster a welcoming committee, hadn't we?'

The Headmaster cast his eye around the boys lolling on the grass, cheering on their team. He settled on two chaps engrossed in their electronic games. Ghastly things, thought the Headmaster. Anti-social in the extreme, and typical of these two, drop-outs of the third form, totally unable to fit in with the pack. No good at games, not team players. Barely spoke, even to each other.

'Tavallali and Green Minor,' called out the Headmaster, prodding them with the sharp end of his shooting-stick. 'You two look as though you could do with some exercise. Come with me, please. And turn those things off before I confiscate them.'

And off they went, the welcoming committee.

So far, Magnus had not felt very welcome. No sign of Mother at the airport, no semblance of a conversation from the taxi-driver, a locked gate, and, to cap it all, a head-on assault by a guided missile that might have caused brain damage. He picked at the crater-sized dent that the ball had left on his trunk. M. GOVE was now M. G VE.

Magnus plopped down on to the offended object, and looked around. The sight did not make him feel any happier. There, looming behind the trees like a great rhinoceros, was a tall building that seemed to stretch up into the sky. The grey-black stone base was piled high with turrets, and a sloping roof was peppered with attic window upon attic window, almost to the clouds. Jutting out at all angles, with cruel faces of pain and dismay, were literally hundreds of stone gargoyles. Gargoyles were medieval creatures intended to ward off evil spirits, Father had said, when they went round the Cathedral of Notre-Dame together. Magnus could not understand how anyone would want something so horrid-looking around them. And he certainly couldn't understand it now. In all of Magnus's ten years of travelling from city to city with Father, this place did not look like any hotel he had ever seen.

Then he spotted the Headmaster making his way to where he sat on his trunk. He was wearing tailor-made country attire (more managing director than headmaster, he liked to think). His large round face above the huge bow-tie got larger and larger, filling Magnus's field of vision completely, looking very much like a concierge who knows he's in for a generous tip.

'Dr Gove, I presume,' bellowed the Headmaster,

lifting Magnus off his feet with such a powerful pump of the hand that the little chap gave a small squeal. Back down on terra firma, Magnus asked the Headmaster to repeat this curious greeting. It wasn't that it wasn't loud enough (for it most certainly was), but rather that Magnus was not, nor had he ever been, a doctor: 'I'm sorry, I didn't catch that?'

'Yes, Dr Gove, I presume.' The Headmaster couldn't believe that an English boy would not be familiar with his little reference to the famous greeting between those great Victorian explorers, Stanley and Dr Livingstone, when they met in the middle of deepest Africa. Magnus and the Headmaster stared at each other for a moment with that bemused look that indicates things have not really got off on the right foot. Brought up to cover these embarrassing cracks in conversation, Magnus piped up, 'Well, actually, it's Magnus Gove.'

The Headmaster's beam dimmed a little, and he shook his head warily in response: 'Yes, of course.' Yet another joke gone unappreciated. His wife had often said that he had only become a schoolteacher because nobody else laughed at his feeble jokes. He pressed on:

'I am the Headmaster.' Surely that was clear enough. Magnus nodded and smiled politely. Communication at last.

'Your mother telephoned to say that she wouldn't be able to meet you at Heathrow. Delayed in Monte Carlo apparently, some shoot or other . . . shame, shame . . .' He tailed off, trying to picture the grouse moors of Monaco. Then, noticing that Magnus's face had dropped, he went on, 'Anyway, here you are.'

As if by magic, he pulled two boys from behind his back. Magnus had not even noticed them, but then again, by the nervous look of them, they might not be noticed at their own birthday parties.

'These,' continued the Headmaster, 'are Tavallali and Green Minor. They're going to take you to your dormitory.'

Without more ado, the two boys, who Magnus thought bore a striking resemblance to Laurel and Hardy, brushed past him and hoisted up one end of the trunk. Tavallali was 'Hardy', a generously proportioned fellow of indeterminable Middle Eastern origins squeezed into grey trousers, shirt and tie that he had outgrown a few years earlier. Green Minor was a spindly chap with lank hair dripping over his huge glasses and huge unfocused eyes. Funny name, Minor, thought Magnus. Neither of them said hello, but simply teetered with the trunk, pushing it into the backs of Magnus's legs. Magnus heaved up his end and off they went, an awkward six-legged mass of bandy legs and puffing cheeks.

The Headmaster watched the little parade move off, and called after them, partly for Magnus's benefit, but mainly to hear his own majestic voice dominating the surroundings once more: 'Bit awkward arriving so late in the term, but I think you'll be happy here, Gove. We're just one big family . . .'

Magnus looked back and attempted a smile, but Tavallali and Green Minor blocked his view. The Headmaster continued his speech for his own benefit: 'Oh yes, just one big happy family. And the bigger the better.' He rubbed his hands together, then bent down to pick up a shiny 10-pence coin he noticed on the ground, first making sure no one was watching. After all, a penny found is a penny earned. Or was it a penny saved? Whatever.

Meanwhile, Magnus was being pulled along by his two reluctant guides through the great stone doorway and into a cavernous hall that was all the more imposing for its emptiness. The only watching eyes belonged to a couple of stuffed moose heads, dusty and frayed around the antlers.

When they reached the towering staircase, the two pullers of the trunk barely pulled, forcing Magnus to bear the full weight up the steep incline. Being polite, he didn't complain, but instead attempted to make conversation with his new-found compatriots.

'Do you like it here?' puffed Magnus as they climbed.

Tavallali and Green Minor looked at each other with utter disbelief at the stupidity of the question. 'Like it?' exclaimed Tavallali. 'Nobody *likes* it here.' Not much of a start, thought Magnus, but he pressed on. 'How long have you been here?'

'Yonks,' said Tavallali with feeling.

'How long is a yonk?' asked Magnus.

Green Minor jumped in, as if his speaking function had just been switched on: 'Two years, two terms, three weeks, five days . . .' and, looking at the arm holding the nearest bit of the trunk, with its oversized, multi-coloured LCD watch with a picture of Goofy on it, ' . . . seventeen hours, twelve minutes, six . . .'

'Oh shut up, Goof!' barked Tavallali.

'At least *I'm* not Tava the Hut . . .' snarled Green Minor, puffing out his cheeks to make a fat face, based loosely, Magnus supposed, on Jabba the Hutt. These two were clearly not the best of friends. Within seconds they were at each other with the ferocity reserved for seemingly indestructible small boys. All of which was surprising enough to Magnus, who had rarely witnessed such a display, but even more surprising was the fact that they had let go of his trunk twenty steps up the staircase in order to concentrate on their fight. What goes up must come down, especially when it's heavy.

Magnus teetered on the stairs, his face going purple with the effort of holding his trunk steady. He tried signalling to the two gladiators, but they weren't watching. Tavallali had Green Minor's tongue between his fingers and was pulling as hard as he could in an apparent attempt to remove it from his mouth. So the trunk slid downhill, and Magnus had a choice: to be run over or to get on board.

He got on board, and took off like a shot, catapulting down the stairs, with eyes bulging and a scream that never had time to climb out of his open mouth before THUD! Magnus plus trunk hit the bottom. And survived in one piece, thanks to a soft landing on a huge mound of towels, pillowcases, and clothes that had just been neatly ironed and folded. Magnus peeped curiously out of this cloth mountain, still shrieking. This sweet-smelling laundry hadn't been there a few minutes ago, when they started up the stairs. Then another shriek, on a much higher note, took over. It didn't come from up above. Those two were now dangling off the banister, and Green Minor had his fingers up Tava's nose, trying to reach his brain. No, it came from beside him, under the laundry. He peeled back a duvet cover and there she was. An old woman, probably about twenty, thought Magnus. Screaming her lungs out into hands clenched over her face.

Magnus never forgot his good manners: 'I'm very sorry. Are you all right?'

'It's OK. It's OK,' was all that came out between the sobs, and Magnus could just make out tiny frightened eyes behind plastic National Health glasses, and lank greasy hair that was covering a spotty face. Before he could get a better look, the woman dropped her head and busied herself with gathering up the pile of washing.

'Let me help you,' offered Magnus as he handed over a pair of yellowed underpants.

'No, no, please don't,' she stammered, and before Magnus could say any more, she was up on thin, sparrow-like legs, scurrying away up the stairs, past the two combatants, who had now stopped fighting to see what was going on. They came down the stairs slowly, wary of each other. Stalemate.

'Pax?' muttered Green Minor.

'Pax,' replied Tavallali grudgingly, and they set about lifting up the trunk once again.

Magnus, meanwhile, was far away in thought. Maybe it was just his imagination, but he could have sworn that somewhere beneath those glasses and that hair were the most exquisite green eyes he'd ever seen. And just for one second, yes, he was sure now, at that first moment of impact, they had sparkled.

'Who was that?' asked Magnus, staring after the retreating shape of the woman.

'Who?' responded Tava, dismissively.

'That woman.'

Green Minor barely cast her a backward glance. 'Oh, that's Miss Charlotte, she's the under-matron, but she's –'

'Nobody talks to her,' butted in Tavallali.

'Why not?' Magnus was really intrigued now.

Tavallali shrugged. 'Just don't.'

And that was the end of that. So on pressed Magnus with his welcoming committee. Up flights and flights of stairs, over dizzying drops to the worn flagstones below. The chicken-wire around the top balustrade hinted at some terrible accident years before, when high spirits had turned menacingly low. The back stairs led into a rabbit warren of rooms and passageways that gave Magnus a glimpse of what was to come: long, long wooden floors reeking of polish, punctuated only by sturdy iron beds, rooted to the spot; and dingy bathrooms that announced themselves with their communal odour and the hissing of cisterns and washerless taps, long before they ever came into view.

The entire building was totally devoid of life. There were no friendly faces to cheer Magnus along, beckon him in, offer him a little pastry with a café au lait. Magnus wasn't to know that at prep schools all over England, afternoons meant 'All Out', and anyone caught indoors faced serious punishment. Unless it was raining, in which case the masters' wrath would descend on boys breaking the 'All In' rule. Today, like most days of an English summer, it was grey and flat, but not raining. So all there was inside the building was the plop plop of his guides' shoes hurrying down this endless maze to what the Headmaster had referred to as 'his' dormitory.

'Small Boys.' That's what it said on the door, and Magnus could only assume that somewhere else in the building was the rather scary notion of Big Boys. In they piled, past the peeling red gloss door and into Magnus's new home, quite unlike the apartment, with his cosy little bed surrounded by his books, his little desk and the large spinning globe that had once been Father's.

No, this was a huge vaulted room, with a ceiling far up in the rafters where burnt-out lightbulbs hung down on long spindly flexes. On one wall were twelve dressing-gowns with their cords, and below each one was a neatly arranged pair of slippers. A dozen identical black-iron beds stretched into the distance, each tightly made with a grey blanket, and topped with a small pile of freshly laundered blue shirts, black socks and little underpants. The only signs of individuality were tartan rugs of every conceivable shade draped over the beds' ends, and the posters on the walls of super cars, supermodels and cricket stars, all beaming their prowess on to their absent admirers.

There were so many questions Magnus wanted

to ask, like where was he supposed to sleep, and how did he order breakfast, but just as his mouth opened, he was cut short by a deafening bell that was either being rung inside his eardrum or was the loudest bell in the whole world. He spun round to see Tavallali and Green Minor gasp at the noise (this confirmed it as the largest bell in the world – years of familiarity did not seem to make it any less terrifying), their eyes snapped to their watches, they freed their hands from the trunk and ran.

Green Minor was first out of the door, blazing a trail of awkward legs and wheeling arms. Tavallali followed, really quite quickly for a large boy. Whatever that bell meant, thought Magnus, it meant do something quickly. Which he would happily do, if he just knew what on earth it was. Since he didn't, he stood in the middle of Small Boys, and decided to do what any self-respecting young chap who had just arrived at a new hostelry would do: get out of his travelling clothes and dress appropriately for dinner.

He found his bed easily enough, since it had his name printed above it on a small wooden plaque. How kind to put him near the bathroom. Click, cur-lunk went the shiny brass locks on his dented trunk, and from on top of the brand-new folded clothes, each expertly nametaped and ticked off against the clothes list by Marie-Claire, emerged Magnus's pride and joy: his leather-bound scrapbook, full of Father's recipes and his own cut-out collages of the brightly coloured ingredients. It was the only true memory of home that Magnus had been able to fit in the trunk.

He fished out the remains of the pain au chocolat Vaudron had given him for the journey and popped it into his mouth as a little amuse-gueule – he didn't want to spoil his appetite for his first school dinner, particularly if Dryden was so well noted for its cuisine. He slipped the scrapbook under his pillow, and pulled out that black, unyielding pair of lace-ups to replace his red Converse All-Stars.

3

In Major Longfellow's Absence

Pandemonium didn't even begin to describe the scene as Magnus, uniformed and eager to make friends, made his way down the main corridor of the school. His theory had been to follow the wave of bodies, now 'All In' from games, in the most popular direction, trusting that they would lead him to the dining hall and a cake or two to round off the long day's journey and send him to bed happy. Unfortunately, unlike a colony of ants, boys of all shapes and sizes seemed to be running in all directions at once, invariably preceded by a swinging bat or a hard, face-denting ball.

Green Minor and Tavallali could just about be made out in the throng, but they caught sight of Magnus and evaporated instantly. Probably in a hurry, Magnus mused, and gazed at the silver trophies that blazed down at him from glass cabinets. Rows of photographs of rows of boys with folded arms lined the walls, going back ten, twenty, no, over a hundred years, until the black-and-white pictures were faded beyond recognition. Magnus wondered if somewhere in those frames might be the face of Father, youthful eyes staring out at the world. But then, he thought, Father, like son, was never much of a sportsman. Unless there were photos of the cooking club, Father and son were doomed never to gaze at each other across this particular corridor.

Up ahead, a great whoop went up, and a lot of foot-stamping accompanied cheers of approval. Magnus pushed forward to see what was up, and, as the crowds parted, he came face to face with the dangerous end of a cricket bat flashing through the air. Earlier on it had been a cricket ball that had narrowly missed his ear. Now it was a bat that threatened to take off his nose. Later on it did not surprise Magnus to discover that both missiles had been launched by the very same person: BATHURST, R. R. There he stood, like Magnus ten years old, but a full head taller, with a magnificent mane of dark, wavy hair on a sculpted forehead, a thin aristocratic nose and thin red lips that were permanently turned down at the edges in a grimace of condescension. And at this moment, this was further exaggerated as he gazed down at the new bug, who squirmed blondly in the middle of the corridor. Bathurst's air of effortless superiority was broken by the arrival of the Headmaster at his shoulder, as he came up to him, his star pupil, and clutched him to his side for all to see.

'Ah, Gove,' boomed the Headmaster, instantly silencing the crowd.

Magnus smiled, relieved if nothing else to see a familiar face.

All around, faces of every shape and size craned in to have a look at who or what was worthy of the personal attention of this most important member of staff.

'Blending in nicely,' the Headmaster continued. Then, proudly looking down at his protégé, 'I see you've met Bathurst. You've had rather a good day, well done you.' Bathurst was used to taking compliments. This one needed nothing more than a small nod of thanks. The Headmaster looked round for confirmation and a small ripple of applause from the assembled mob provided it.

'Excellent. Now, why don't you be Gove's nurse for the next couple of weeks, till he gets settled in?' The Headmaster peered down in his most avuncular fashion. 'Think of Bathurst as a sort of older brother. All right? Good, good.' And with that he waltzed down the corridor to greet yet another set of prospective pound signs – whoops – parents, this time newly arrived from Taiwan. Magnus extended his small hand, as Father had always taught him to do.

'Hello. Nice to meet you. I'm Magnus.' Bathurst watched the final stitch of the Headmaster's tweed suit disappear round the corner and then allowed himself to turn. His hands remained firmly on the bat, and his smile muscles were quickly relaxed into the more familiar sneer.

'Oh, really?'

Maybe Bathurst had enough younger brothers to be going on with. But as he marched through the cavernous halls of the school, with Magnus trotting along behind, receiving adulation from every form room, Magnus was grateful for the tour of the building, albeit a lightning one that left him more confused than when he started.

'Form room's here. You're in 3A with us. Your

33

desk's at the back. You pick up stationery from here, after breakfast. Wellingtons on this peg. Got your number on it. What's your number? Games kit here, same number, different peg. Bank here. Hand in all your money at the beginning of term and after exeats to the Bursar. He's the one with the moustache and the dog called Major. Not to be confused with *the* Major. Four houses. Africa, Australia, Canada and India. I'm in Africa.' Bathurst nodded at a cabinet, his house clearly engraved on the glass. Inside was quite a treasure trove: row upon row of cups and trophies of silver and gold.

'You're in India.' Magnus looked up to see just a single, rather small, wooden plaque within.

'Dining hall here. Times for baths, games, rest, reading, lights out and meals on the board. Got it?' Bathurst didn't wait for an answer, especially now that his two-week job had been completed in less than ten minutes. At long last, the dining hall, thought Magnus, as Bathurst led the way into a thunderingly noisy room, rapidly filling with boys, each snatching their own napkins from pigeon-holes and standing behind their allotted spaces at long wooden benches.

'Your napkin. Your responsibility. Lose it and you pay. You any good at cricket?' This time, he did pause, briefly.

'No, I've never played,' said Magnus. Wrong answer.

'Oh well, you'll have to learn. What about tennis?'

'Afraid not,' confessed Magnus. Wrong answer again.

'What *do* you play, then?' Bathurst was now openly contemptuous.

'I like to cook.'

Bathurst let out a sharp laugh that had nothing to do with amusement. 'Cook? Girls cook.'

They arrived at the table in the corner of the room, where Bathurst assumed pole position, leaving no space for Magnus to join him. It was clear that the tour was over, especially when a small hand bell rang out, and the room fell silent. From up on high table where the masters sat came an incantation in a foreign tongue that Magnus had never heard before.

'Benedic Domine nos et haec tua dona quae datur largitate sumus sumpturi, per Iesum Christum Dominum nostrum, Amen.'

Now Magnus was worried. He needed to find his place or he would be the only one left standing when everybody sat down. He finally found a spot, between Tavallali and Green Minor, at what could only be described as the unfashionable part of town. When grace was over, a cacophony of voices broke out, combined with 150 boys crashing down on to the benches, clashing their cutlery and tucking into their meal with the fervour of people who expect never to be fed again.

Magnus was inevitably slow off the mark. Partly out of inexperience, but more out of sheer horror at the food that lay on his plate. Not that Magnus was expecting a feast. A little contrefilet with a nice salad, or even a croque monsieur would have done. But instead he was faced with a gelatinous off-white

Magnus's Crêpes au Sucre et au Citron

(Makes 20 small crêpes)

For the crêpes:
150g plain flour
3 large eggs
475 ml full-fat milk
90g unsalted butter

For the filling:
butter
fine zest of 1 lemon
icing sugar

1. Sift the flour into a mixing bowl.
2. Make a well in the centre of the flour and break the eggs into it.
3. Stir the eggs gradually incorporating the flour to make a batter and slowly adding the milk to keep the mixture liquid.
4. Melt the butter in a saucepan. Add it to the batter and stir well.
5. Allow the batter to stand in the refrigerator for at least 20 minutes.

6 Lightly whip the batter again to break up any lumps of flour. Transfer the batter to a jug.

7 Melt some more butter in a crêpe pan (or a heavy frying pan) and make sure it covers the whole surface. Heat the pan until it is very hot.

8 For each crêpe pour about 1/4 cup of batter into the centre of the pan. Tilt the pan in all directions until the batter is spread evenly reaching every side of the pan. Cook for about 1 minute.

9 Loosen the edges of the crêpe with a palette knife and then turn the crêpe over. Cook for a further 30 seconds.

10 Sprinkle the lemon zest on to the crêpe and add sugar to taste. Fold the crêpe in half and fold again to serve.

Magnus's tips: Don't pile the finished crêpes on top of each other as I do in the film, because they will stick together. If you can't serve them straight away, fold them over and lay them out.

Very often the first crêpe will stick to the pan, and tear when you try to turn it over. Don't worry: after that one it's much easier!

pâté stained by the unmistakable purple of beetroot, which had also overflowed on to half a baked potato that had gone hard. He prised the potato away from the infectious red colour and searched around for some butter and pepper to improve the situation. At that moment Tavallali scooped the final slush of butter out of its tin platter, which he clanged down beside Magnus. He would have to be brave.

'Excuse me. Is there any more butter?' Magnus asked tentatively.

Tavallali and Green Minor shook their heads as they continued to shovel the red mess into their stained mouths. Green Minor came out with something, his mouth impossibly full.

Tavallali chimed in with further elucidation through another huge forkload: 'No, but there's marge. It's polyunsaturated. Forty-four calories less per serving.

'Headman says it's good for us. Why don't you go and get some more?'

Magnus didn't really hear the titters run around the 3A table as he hauled himself up off the bench and carried the butter dish ahead of him towards the great swing doors of the school kitchen. Like young Master Twist approaching Mr Bumble for a second helping, everybody but he knew his fate. Passing the sign that proclaimed: 'OUT OF BOUNDS TO ALL BOYS', he eased himself through the portals and into that great hearth of any English institution: the kitchen.

Unlike the male-dominated kitchens of the Parisian restaurants his father had introduced him to, this was a bustling, steaming workhouse filled entirely by women, with raw sausage fingers and heavy breasts covered by pristine white aprons. So occupied were they with their chopping and boiling that they hardly noticed this intrusion, and Magnus was afraid to disturb their devoted labour. Instead he weaved onwards past racks of brown and grey vegetables: cabbages of every hue, parsnips, turnips, swedes, leeks and finally the unmistakable dark blotches of soil-hardened beetroots. Unlike the market, this was a gastronomic nadir, devoid of colour. Or smell. With its shiny surfaces and metallic containers, this kitchen reminded Magnus more of the hospital where Father was.

And suddenly he was stopped by someone who looked like the doctor. This was the school Chef, a lone, slight male beating a fast and furious path towards him, waving a very large metal spoon. His face was white, either from fury or from too many years spent at catering college in sunless Kent, and his hair was pressed close to his head by a lime-green hairnet.

'No, no, no, no, no. No boys allowed in here. Fire hazard, health hazard. Just a hazard hazard.' He was right next to Magnus now, more astonished than angry that this small boy should have penetrated so far into his kingdom. But not half as astonished as Magnus, whose mouth hung wide open.

'What do you want anyway?' Chef demanded.

Magnus found a small voice. 'Some more margarine?'

Chef's eyes bulged, but even he could see from

the empty butter dish that this was a reasonable request. He considered it for a brief moment, and then burst back into frenetic life.

'Yes, yes, yes, yes.' And, turning abruptly on his heel, he catapulted off towards the central cooking station, bouncing around the room like a ball in a pinball machine, waving his spoon and wiping surfaces as he went. Magnus took this as a cue to follow, but was instantly stopped in his tracks by Chef's machine-gun-fire commands.

'Don't come in, don't come in, don't come in. Beryl, where's the I Can't Believe It's Not Butter?' Beryl responded and Chef rushed back to Magnus, offering a new dish, filled with margarine moulded into a precise pattern.

'There you are. Whoops.' To complete the beauty of the dish, he popped a sprig of parsley dead centre and smoothed it down with the nib of his little finger. Pleased that his creation, however humble, was ready to greet the mouths of the world, he resumed his frantic gesticulation.

'Now go, go, go, go, go. Go.' And when Magnus had retreated back through the doors, unsure what to make of this extraordinary repeater of words in a hairnet, Chef brushed his hands together and exclaimed 'Gone!'

Back at the 3A table, Bathurst observed the potential for a spot of fun. Fun at somebody else's expense. And who better than the new bug, the collective hatred of whom would always confirm his own position as top dog? Not that he needed such displays. As brightest boy in the class, top athlete and best bred, his pinnacle was secure, but entertaining diversions for the masses were what his father had always classed as good public relations.

He nodded to his henchman, Mee, who was a particularly violent chap whose diminutive stature and lowly breeding had been honed into a pure aggression of which Bathurst entirely approved. Richard Mee (who was destined later in life to become a property developer known as Dick Mee) was just the right kind for a number two bully. Fast bowler, terrific on the left wing, and no fool when it came to practical subjects, he was nevertheless a powerful force much in need of subtle guidance to be truly sinister. Bathurst wanted to take his time thinking up something appropriately sinister for Gove, but in the meantime, why not start with something simply cruel?

Mee received his unspoken orders with a toothy grin, leaned across the length of the table, elbowing the more passive specimens of 3A out of the way, and unzipped a pencil case. Apart from the ink stains that covered it and its owner, it was fairly unthreatening as a weapon, were it not for its non-stationery, and unstationary, contents: a gnawing, pinching army of giant ants he had sent off for from an exotic pet delivery service. These were Peruvian soldier ants, and anybody who is familiar with ants knows that these buggers have pincers the size and sharpness of garden shears and a less than priestly disposition. They dropped on to Magnus's unattended salad, and, within seconds of disengaging themselves from their parachute landing, they headed off into what must have seemed to them to be very jungle-like territory. The whole table could hardly contain themselves behind their snot-covered sleeves.

The victim reappeared. Magnus was quite pleased with himself at having brought back a full margarine dish for everybody else to share. It was a small offering for his new-found colleagues, soon to be friends, he was sure. He sat down and scooped up a dollop, transferring it triumphantly to his potato. But he should have used his ears more than his eyes. The hush of anticipation that held the table to such rapt attention would have given the game away even to a novice. But Magnus saw only the prospect of food at last, and tucked into his marge-slithered cold, hard potato with a lettuce leaf for garnish.

The burning sensation that followed was quite unforgettable. Something had taken hold of his tongue with a saw and was drawing blood. He spat out what was in his mouth, but still the agony wouldn't go away. Sure enough, as everybody else could see to their great amusement, a lone soldier ant was clinging ferociously to the end of Magnus's outstretched tongue, piercing its way into the bloody flesh. It was all Magnus could do not to scream his lungs out, but the mirth around him was too obvious to allow him to give them the satisfaction. Instead he picked up the jug of water beside him, and drowned the blighter. Ants are not amphibious. Just as the audience's appreciation reached its climax, the Headmaster's bell went and his voice reached across the room. 'Silence, please!'

3A stopped laughing, except Mee, who was so tickled by his genius that he erupted into an even more uncontrolled fit of hysteria.

'Mr Mee,' singled out the Headmaster, 'would you care to share the joke with us?' Only then did Mee clamp his hands over his head and block every orifice that might release a giggle. 'Now then, in Major Longfellow's absence, I have the pleasure of congratulating the following on being awarded their colours. Horbye in Canada House.' The perfunctory clapping ran around the room, and an older boy raised his fist into the air. 'And Kessell in Australia House, both from the First XI.' More polite claps from the younger boys, and admiring glances from masters still dressed in minor. county cricket sweaters.

'And from Africa,' the Headmaster proceeded, 'with another outstanding century against Wakeley Court this afternoon, Bathurst in the Colts.' The room erupted in applause, admiring those of true physical excellence. Even the senior boys paid due acknowledgement to their junior compatriot for whom it was only a matter of time until he would be equally successful in the Firsts. But none clapped as heartily as the 3A table, led by Mee. Had Magnus been watching closely he might have wondered whether they were clapping out of devotion or fear. But he was far too busy fighting off an ant who was on a mission in his shorts.

4

You Can All Thank Bathurst

Magnus's first night in the dormitory was at least some respite from the horrors of the dining hall. He was propelled along by bells and the ebb and flow of boys who knew where they were going. He followed Tavallali from a discreet but steady distance, because he assumed that he would be heading in the right direction and he was hard to miss in the crowd. After washing his face, hanging up his flannel and towel in the bathroom, and checking his name on the once-a-week bath list, he made for the relative safety of his bed, checking that his scrapbook was still under his pillow. Then something most unusual happened. Unusual for him, anyway. A giant pillow fight started.

From his vantage point by the door, Magnus had watched the whole thing brewing. Surreptitiously, Mee crept up to the huge door that stood closed at the near end of the dormitory. It wasn't a door that was used for coming and going, and it was too large to be a cupboard, so Magnus had assumed it to be a hangover from bygone days, now painted shut. But then why did the ancient wooden plaque fixed to it carry the crumbling gold-leafed name MAJOR V. E. LONGFELLOW? And surely that was a name he recognized from supper time? The Headmaster had mentioned it. 'In Major Longfellow's absence . . .'

Now he came to think about it, the name had resounded down the corridors ever since Magnus had arrived. That and the odd name Raptor. Apparently neither was around, and their absences seemed to cause boys and masters alike to be lighter of spirit than they might otherwise have been. Magnus took note to watch out for their return.

So there hovered Mee, beside a grotesque and clumsily painted poster of *Jurassic Park*, which Magnus had been taken to see by Father after much resistance. Father had dragged his heels all summer, disliking anything that smacked of popular culture, but Magnus had finally prevailed. After all, there's nothing worse than not having seen the film that everybody else, even Marie-Claire, had seen.

Rather cleverly, somebody had painted over the 'Jurassic' on the poster and replaced it with 'Dryden'. The dinosaur had also been given a scholar's mortar board and a billowing pipe that hung from its jaws. Mee leaned down over the plaque on the door and covered V. E. LONGFELLOW with V. E. LOCIRAPTOR. Slowly, all became clear to Magnus. Longfellow and Raptor were one and the same. Gulp. They were ten times as talked about together as they were individually, and now that he recognized the reference they took on seriously terrifying proportions. Worse than that, this Raptor person, wherever he was now, clearly lived behind that huge door, right by Magnus's bed. Magnus tried not to think about it too much.

Luckily, he was distracted by a pillow whooshing

through the air and slamming Mee's head into the oak doorframe. Bathurst then marched away, whistling with innocence. Mee picked himself up, rubbing both the back and front of his head, and narrowed his eyes in search of the perpetrator. He found something much more promising: a target. Green Minor was reuniting his teddy bear's body with its head after he had found it hanging from a noose above his bed. Mee came at him, bursting out of nowhere, and slammed the pillow that had hit him straight into Green Minor's neck. Green Minor went flying. Upper and lower halves of teddy did the same. A war cry rang out from Bathurst's corner, and the whole dormitory descended from the hills like the Assyrian upon the fold (whatever they were – Magnus could only remember that one line from the poem).

The battle that ensued was an astonishing display of hand-to-hand combat, reminiscent of the days of knights in armour. With pillows as broadswords, Bathurst and Mee took up the higher ground on Green Minor's bed, fighting off the advances of the 3A infantry. The pair held their position magnificently. Bathurst with long, powerful strokes, and Mee with deadly staccato fire, easily defied the long-held military theory that defenders with less than half the number of attackers were likely to lose their ground. Here in Small Boys, the Zulus were entirely unable to defeat those brave Men of Harlech at Rorke's Drift. Green Minor, whose bed was the territory in dispute, cowered underneath it, trying to rescue his dismembered teddy. Tavallali kept out

of the fray completely, applying mousse to his luxur-
iant black hair.

Magnus watched in increasing horror. Surely
somebody would be killed. One boy, whom he later
learned was Luerssen Major, was on the wrong end
of a Bathurst strike and was thrown backwards on
to an old cast-iron radiator. His head hit first and
made a crack that must have resounded through all
128 rooms of Dryden Park. His hand reached up
and came away covered in blood, but nobody
seemed to care. He started to cry, and even as he
attempted to get to the door somebody knocked
him down again. Magnus was about to try and help
him when Miss Charlotte came scurrying in, wringing her hands at the sight of Luerssen's obvious
brain damage and the general scene of destruction.

'Stop it!' she wailed. It was supposed to be an
authoritative shout, but her voice simply was not
up to it. All that could be heard was the noise of
bed springs, pillows connecting with heads, and
heads hitting walls. 'I said stop it now! I'll report
you to Major Longfellow!'

Bathurst heard that one, and shouted back defi-
antly, 'Raptor's not here!' Hear hear, agreed the
rest of them, joining the rallying cry.

'Raptor's not here! Raptor's not here!'

Charlotte had played her trump card, and it had
failed miserably. Her eyes blinked furiously, and her
fringe kept getting in the way. She knew she couldn't
retreat. But she couldn't advance either. She simply
boiled inside, and shook outside. Then she got hit,
full in the face, her glasses ramming into her nose. She

lost all semblance of control. Only Magnus could see rage rising up through her body, and then out it came, in a terrific bellow: 'BLOODY WELL STOP IT!'

There was a cease-fire. Even these wild boys were ashamed to have provoked such a vehement response. After all, they were boys who faintly recalled mothers and sisters. 3A stood silently. Then, without looking at Charlotte or at each other, they sloped back to their beds, pretending nothing had happened. All except Bathurst, for whom dominance of weaker vessels was essential to his social standing. He drew himself up to his full height on the bed and looked down at Charlotte, who was thoroughly shocked now by her own outburst. A thin smile on his face, he loosened his dressing-gown cord to reveal blue-striped pyjama bottoms below his muscular torso. She blushed visibly, but stood her ground. Then he placed his hands on his hips and thrust them forward in a lewd gesture, accompanied by a phrase only known to prep-school boys: '*Pwang!*'

Charlotte visibly shrank, and bit into her lip, looking for escape. Too late. The boys, like hyenas, scented blood and moved in for the kill.

'*Pwang!*' went Bathurst again, thrusting towards her face.

'*Pwang! Pwang! Pwang!*' they all chanted, standing on their beds, eleven boys in unison, shoving themselves at the poor girl, cornered by their crude expression of something they knew almost nothing about. Magnus noticed that even Green Minor had come out from his hiding place to push his decapitated teddy's sexless lower half at Charlotte. This was no longer the cuddly teddy who kept out the draughts in bed, this was a demon teddy with horns and a curly tail. They were all devils. That's it, thought Magnus, entranced by this hateful ritual, they are demons in disguise.

The spell was broken only when the Headmaster strolled in.

'Small Boys!' he bellowed with the benevolent bark of an old general, who expects chaps to behave like chaps despite the rules and regulations. And so they reverted to small boys, bouncing down on to the floor noisily, full of playfulness and innocence, theatrically picking up the musty striped pillows that had slipped out of their cases. A few feathers floated down from above. The Headmaster brushed one from his tweedy shoulder as he approached Magnus's bed, his smile shifting from reproval to benevolence. Always important to head off newcomers' blues before they made panicked telephone calls to their parents and upset the balance sheet.

'Settling in all right, are we?' he inquired.

'Yes, thank you, sir,' came Magnus's automatic response. Why is it that we never answer truthfully to those social platitudes? But the Headmaster took it all at face value.

'Splendid. Probably a livelier bunch than you're used to at home, eh?' And off he trailed as he scrutinized the dormitory, who were all chatting away, trying to postpone the moment of lights out. The Headmaster, barely concealing his irritation, reassumed control with his deepest voice. 'Gentlemen, I take it we're all agreed that the absence of

Major Longfellow doesn't mean that we're not all going to be very quiet now, does it?' He reached for the light switch beside Raptor's door, and waited, hand poised. The boys let out elaborate yawns and snores to confirm that they were indeed going straight to sleep and wouldn't need any monitoring that night. It was part of the game that he should pretend to be fooled. He gave Magnus a final wink, and plunged them all into darkness.

'Good-night. Lights out.' And off padded his soft shoes, squeaking down the corridor.

As Magnus's eyes adjusted to the dark, he could make out shapes moving in the dorm. Shapes with no sound. He eased himself deeper under the safety of his covers, only the whites of his eyes showing, large and very concerned. Were they coming for him, out of the gloom, from all sides, to attack him with pillows – or worse? But nobody came. The shapes materialized not as aggressors, but dancing shadows on the walls, and just there, yes, lurking behind those shadows, a snarling face with its shiny teeth.

A bright light flashed on, beaming in from the window, to reveal the face of the dinosaur, mortar board, pipe and all. And it was staring directly at Magnus. The light moved around the room. There was a crunch of gravel outside, and the throaty roar of an old diesel motor car. The tyres swerved and ground to a halt. The diesel spluttered, the lights were killed and the door of the car swung open. Out stepped the largest and shiniest black Oxford shoes in England. Magnus's instinct had been correct. There was definitely evil afoot.

Magnus, in the meantime, could see only feet when his world was, literally, turned upside-down. They had come out of the darkness with no warning, except the sound of Bathurst's voice barking, 'Lamppost!' The far end of the bed where Magnus's feet were was suddenly lifted up, bringing both his feet and his mattress curling down over his head. And to add insult to injury, he couldn't orientate himself thanks to a bank of blinding torch lights waving in front of his eyes. They were so close he could hear the batteries humming. Then the interrogation began.

'Why have you come so late?'

'Where are you from?'

'What does your dad do?'

'Why are you so weedy?'

'Have you had a bath yet?'

'What's the square root of 112?'

'Come on, say something, you little maggot.' That sounded like Bathurst. Magnus found it hard to reply while his toenails were sticking into his nostrils. Luckily another voice chimed in.

'Cave! Cave! Raptor!'

This was met with groans of derision from the assembled inquisitors.

'Yeah! Raptor won't be back for ages yet.' Mee's south London drawl was unmistakable.

The door blasted open. Not just any door, but the huge one beyond which evil lay. The torches and their bearers fled, and were back in bed snoring their individual heads off by the time the lights came on. Which was immediately. Magnus unscrewed his eyes to see an upside-down room. Hanging from the floor above him were a pair of enormously black shoes atop stiff dark-grey trousers. They advanced on him like a military unit, clicking metal against the polished floor. The iron bedstead groaned and great shavings of wooden floor flew as his bed was returned to its horizontal plane. It thumped on to the floor, and Magnus peeped up at his saviour. He looked up and up, further and further until he reached a face, way up there, almost reaching the rafters. A great square chin, a shock of white hair scraped back from a noble forehead. And beneath jet black eyebrows that curled up at the ends, the deepest, blackest eyes Magnus had ever seen. Major V. E. Longfellow (rtd), late of Her Majesty's Royal Artillery, based at Bovington Camp, Dorset, was back. Magnus was face to face with Raptor.

'Ah, the new boy. How predictable of you all.' No smile. Raptor turned on his heel and marched in long strides down the full length of the dormitory, eyes front, chin up. You couldn't hear a spring creak. Nothing.

'Perhaps you would care to predict what I am about to do?'

Total and absolute silence.

'Anyone?'

No.

'Tavallali?'

Tavallali gulped. 'Lines, sir?'

Raptor did not bother to acknowledge that suggestion.

'The punishment having been decided, the question remains therefore: how many?' He wheeled suddenly and towered over Goof.

'Green Minor?' Goof sat up in a panic, and fumbled around on his bedside table to gather his spectacles and a battered old notebook with an elastic band round it. With the glasses hanging off one ear, and the elastic band flicking across the room, he found the right place in the book, and cleared his throat as quietly as possible.

'Well, sir, your average this term is . . . 181, sir. So 150?' It was a risk of which any young negotiator would have been proud. Magnus was impressed by Goof's guts. Raptor, on the other hand, wasn't such an easy touch.

'Surely you would not expect me to fall below my average? Bathurst, how did you do today?'

Bathurst spoke modestly but clearly from his trophy-strewn corner: '117 not out, sir.' Raptor smiled for the first time. Not a smile as we understand a smile to be, but a parting of the thin lips that revealed a crack in the armour.

'Hmm. Then 117 it is, and you can all thank Bathurst for that.'

5

A Most Inconsiderate Boy

'Bathurst!'

Raptor's voice shot through the 3A form room to Bathurst's temple. The oak-panelled classroom had been the library when the school was still a stately home, and it was still very imposing. Leather-bound books propped up ancient busts of lesser-known philosophers, and maps of the Roman Empire proclaimed quite clearly that this was now a room for classical learning. Raptor had insisted on keeping his blackboard, eschewing the current fashion, and the Headmaster's pleas, for overhead projectors (doubtless based on some vulgar 'deal' he was doing). Raptor knew that some of the staff thought he was old-fashioned, but as far as he, Major Victor E. Longfellow, was concerned, his was the *only* fashion.

Bathurst strolled to the front of the class and deposited his lines on a large oak desk. Over by the window, facing away from the class, Raptor stood in his long black gown. His voice continued to call the roll in a measured expectation of obedience. He didn't need to look at anyone. Magnus watched with a certain detachment. These were the names of boys that, as yet, were not real people to him.

'Burkhart, Cubitt, Green Minor, Luerssen Major, Mee, Merriman, Oberoi, Pears, Tavallali,

Williams.' Raptor paused and cleared his throat in a way that Magnus would come to know so well. 3A had all resumed their seats. The lines were piled neatly on the table. The birds twittered away merrily in the Italianate gardens outside. Magnus wondered what would happen next.

'And Gove, M. Ten years, one month.'

That was him. He piped up. 'Sir.'

Raptor's ears scanned the room seeking the patter of a small boy's shoes and the flop of lines upon lines, but he failed to detect it.

'Gove?'

'Here, sir.'

Raptor twitched. Invisible antennae were hard at work. 'I can see that. What I can't see are your lines.'

'I haven't done any.'

3A took a very deep breath, and outside the window the birds stopped in mid-song. Very slowly, like an oil tanker turning, Raptor swivelled to face the class.

'You. Haven't. Done. Any.'

'I haven't done anything wrong,' whispered Magnus. He was aware that around him, boys' heads were shaking, their bottoms shifting away from him on their desk benches.

Raptor's calm finally broke. 'Yes, you have,' he roared, 'you didn't listen.' Raptor sailed down the room, scraping his long, hairy fingers across the desks as he passed. Each one showed gouge marks afterwards.

'While I doubt that you were wholly responsible

for lampposting your own bed it is my task to instil in you a sense of community. Great empires were founded on this tradition, Gove, and I will not tolerate its erosion here in 3A!' Raptor's eyebrows were now less than three inches away from Magnus's cowering face.

Magnus quivered, but he was saved by the proverbial bell. It rang, and Raptor slowly drew himself up to his full height once more. 3A had still not moved.

'However, I shall make an allowance this once. And in case you thought I'd forgotten, the Thursday Test this week will be on the pluperfect subjunctives of irregular verbs.' Groans all round. Raptor had made his point. It was going to be a stinker of a test.

The first weeks of Magnus's life at Dryden Park were the unhappiest of his life. He missed Father. He waited patiently in the scrum that surrounded Raptor every time the post came. But he always remained the only one standing beside an empty-handed Raptor, who told him to go back to his desk and practise his irregulars. With every day that passed, Magnus forgot little things about Father. The grey on his temples was probably white by now, he guessed. Maybe he hadn't survived his operation, and nobody had come to tell him. Maybe Marie-Claire was dead too. Maybe no one knew that he was here. The darkness of despair grew.

On top of this the shock of alien activities such a cricket and Latin were disturbing enough, but the absence of edible food was intolerable. Day after day, Chef and his busy team of busty women produced dishes that pushed back the known barriers of greyness.

On one occasion Magnus tried to send back the oozing off-white square that slid on to his plate from Raptor's serving spoon. In any ordinary restaurant, he knew, the waiters happily took things back. But even Magnus was coming to realize that Dryden was no ordinary anything.

Raptor elbowed the dish back at Magnus. 'Don't be wet, Gove. It'll put hairs on your chest.'

Raptor was adamant that everything that was served should be eaten. He had heard that some of the young masters allowed boys on their tables to have a small portion of dishes they didn't like, but he would have none of it. You never knew where the next ration was coming from; it was for their own good. It certainly wasn't because Raptor was a great fan of Chef's cuisine himself. In fact this lunchtime, Raptor thought, Chef had really outdone himself. The plate in front of him looked like nothing he had ever seen before.

Raptor called Chef over, and asked him most politely: 'Ah, Chef. Umm . . . What exactly is this?'

Chef allowed himself a small chuckle of pride. 'Tofu lasagne, Major Longfellow.'

Raptor's face fell a long way, but he concealed his horror very well, Magnus thought. 'Yes . . . Very healthy. Is there any truth to the rumour that there's cheese to look forward to?'

'Oh yes, yes, yes,' giggled Chef. A ray of hope was lit around the table. 'A lovely Greek feta. Semi-skimmed.'

Tava's and Goof's
Sablés au Beurre

(Makes 30 small biscuits)

90g unsalted butter
125g self-raising flour
1 egg yolk
1 tbsp double cream
40g icing sugar
salt

1   Dice the unsalted butter into small cubes and allow to warm to room temperature (about 3 hours).

2   Sift the flour. Repeat twice more, which will make the mixture light and airy.

3   In a large mixing bowl, beat the egg yolk. Add the double cream, icing sugar and a small pinch of salt.

4   Gradually sift in the flour, using your fingertips to create a rough, sandy dough. Be careful not to mix too well.

5   On a floured surface (a chilled marble slab is perfect), work the dough into a ball.

6 Wrap the ball in some clingfilm and refrigerate for at least 1 hour, or overnight if possible.

7 Take the dough out of the fridge 20 minutes before you want to use it to allow it to settle. Preheat the oven to 180°C.

8 With a floured rolling-pin, roll out the dough to an even thickness, about half a centimetre.

9 Cut into desired shapes, using shaped pastry cutters or a pastry knife.

10 Place the biscuits on a greased tray and bake for 20 minutes. Allow to cool before peeling the biscuits off.

Goof's tip: Most kitchens are much warmer than Dryden's. Make sure all your implements are cold, so that the dough doesn't fall apart.

Tava's tip: If you want to make a complicated shape (like a Mercedes Benz 500 SEC), don't bother with too many of the details— they won't come out!

'Oh,' was all Raptor could say.

Magnus buried his head in his hands. He was always hungry.

If there was no nice food to eat, he would have to find some. And find some he did. But in the most peculiar place.

It was a cross-country run on a Tuesday after-noon, and Magnus was at the rear, behind even Tavallali and Green Minor, who tripped over each other's laces and flicked bramble branches on to each other's legs. It was odd, thought Magnus, that although they were both equally useless at anything involving physical effort or coordination, and they were always falling over each other, they had not become friends in any way. They never shared cartridges or blotting paper, let alone the Mars bar that Tavallali produced halfway through the woods. Magnus couldn't believe his eyes. All that sweet, gooey caramel covered with a thick layer of creamy chocolate, nicely softened in Tava's track-suit bot-toms. Alarmingly, it was all fast disappearing down Tava's throat. Magnus could feel the acids in his stomach anticipating chocolate to digest.

'Where did you get that?' implored Magnus. Tava covered the Mars bar with his paw, and narrowed his eyes defensively.

'I saved it from tuck.' Magnus did not know what tuck was, so the explanation didn't help.

'Can I have some?'

'No, wait till tuck on Sunday.'

No sooner had he taken another colossal bite than Raptor leapt out from behind a sturdy oak tree, and whisked the delicacy out of reach. He stood there, in his now rather tight military track-suit and a flat cap, and crushed the bar in his hand.

'When you've quite finished snacking, I expect to see you all at the front with Bathurst.'

'Why, sir?' asked Magnus perplexed.

Raptor was astounded. 'Why? Why? For the same reason that we learn Latin!' And that was all the explanation Magnus was going to get.

Magnus had not been given the opportunity to explain that he suffered from asthma. By the time he reached Surgery after three miles of gruelling uphill struggle, he was half dead, fighting for breath.

Miss Charlotte rubbed soothing oils into his chest and fetched him a new inhaler after he had finished his old one. Slowly, his lungs reflated, and the gasping settled into a gentle wheeze. Miss Charlotte lowered his games shirt, and awkwardly patted him on the shoulders. As a nurse she had been efficient and quietly confident, uttering kind words with a smile of genuine concern. But now that the panic was over she reverted to her old self, acutely aware that Magnus was watching her under the bright strip lights of the cold surgery. Her spots felt especially huge and red today.

'There, feeling better now?' she blurted. 'OK, you can go and get changed.' She edged Magnus off the surgery bed and towards the door. She rejoiced in this rare quiet moment alone as she fished a postcard out of the pocket of her matron's overall. The round, adolescent handwriting on one side and the standard tourist's view of the Arc de Triomphe brought a smile to her face, and she wandered over to a cork board to add it to her collection of postcards from other pen-pals. Beautiful Wiltshire, Ramsgate and Corfe Castle were the prizes of her exotic collection so far, and the picture of Paris went straight to the top. She could just imagine it now. To be as far away as France, that would be wonderful. To get beyond the gates of Dryden would be a start.

'Have you ever been to France?' came a gentle voice behind her. She whipped round in horror. She hated to be surprised. Magnus was sitting back on the bed, his legs swinging casually, his face open and unthreatening. 'We can see that from my father's window.'

'Can you, really?' she said, and then pinched herself for opening up the conversation. In her experience, boys were not to be talked to. It only ever caused trouble in the long run.

'You can come and stay if you like, in the holidays.'

Charlotte twirled her hair around her fingers, tightening it with every turn. 'No. Don't be so silly.'

'I'm not,' answered Magnus, offended by the abrupt dismissal of his invitation. 'My father needs a nurse like you.'

Charlotte, against all her better instincts, found herself being drawn in. She even stepped forward a little. 'What's wrong with him?'

'He's having an operation,' Magnus replied gloomily. But he tried to think positively: 'He's going to get better.' It was his form of prayer.

Charlotte was intrigued by this little boy. He looked just like all the others – ruffled sandy hair, maybe a little small for his age – but there was something different about him. He seemed not to be laughing at her, but to actually want to talk with her. She ventured a bit further.

'What about your mother?' Every boy swanked about his perfect mother. This would be the test.

'She's not around,' said Magnus, passing the test with flying colours. Charlotte had so many questions. They were both looking each other in the eye now. But as she opened her mouth the surgery door bounced open and Miss Plunder thrust her head into the room. She wore an expression that suggested she had just returned from Sodom and Gomorrah, having turned Lot's wife into a pillar of salt.

'Enough idle chatter, Miss Charlotte. Have you finished those name-tapes?'

Charlotte withdrew to her corner, hiding her postcards. 'I was just going to do them now, Miss Plunder.'

'Hrrummph,' went Miss Plunder, knowing full well that people never did anything constructive unless frightened into action. Boys, girls and men all responded to the same treatment. She fixed Magnus with a steely glare. She would have to watch this one very carefully.

In contrast, Magnus firmly believed that this gorgon was to be avoided at all costs. When he discovered that Miss Plunder was the sole distribution outlet for tuck, he was in a dilemma. After lunch on Sunday, the whole school lined up in a regimented, drooling conga, halfway up the grand staircase. At the bottom, fiercely guarding the tuck supply, sat Miss Plunder, doling out one packet of Maltesers to each boy. Unless, of course, they were on the 'Off Tuck' list supplied by the masters, or if the boys' parents had put them on a diet. Magnus fell into neither category, but was convinced that Miss Plunder would find a reason why he shouldn't be allowed his fair share. Time stood still when he finally reached the head of the queue. Maybe there wouldn't be any packets left? He had quite distinctly seen the Bursar make off with a handful after Major had upset the tuck box.

'Gove,' she mused, checking down her lists with her Biro. 'I suppose there's no reason not to let you have some tuck.'

'No, Miss Plunder,' ventured Magnus.

'No tuck,' said Miss Plunder, 'or no reason?'

'No reason,' answered Magnus, unsure. And after a moment's hesitation, as if she were handing over the Crown Jewels for safekeeping, Magnus received the first edible morsel since he had landed in England.

He scuttled out of the hall and let out a whoop, which was quite unlike any sound he had ever made before. But then nothing had given him so much pleasure before. He sped into the classroom to devour the chocolate balls at his leisure, when a leg slammed down across two desks and blocked his passage. He was being held up at the frontier.

'Pay the tariff, Maggot,' demanded Bathurst

lazily, as he sprawled across his desk like a Roman Emperor waiting for his next consignment of grapes. Mee was the owner of the leg-barrier, and it was clearly his job to pick the grapes.

'What tariff?' Magnus inquired. Bathurst had never mentioned this feature during the whistle-stop tour. Mee didn't bother with an explanation. He grabbed the packet, split it open and had poured half of the Maltesers into a secret compartment in his desk before Magnus had a chance to react.

'You can't do that!' Magnus bleated. He didn't mean to bleat, but that's the way it came out.

'Just have,' smiled Bathurst.

'And what are you going to do about it?' shouted Mee, as usual looking for any excuse to get violent. Magnus looked around the form room for help, but 3A was suddenly fully occupied in its letter writing. Magnus suspected that they had been pillaged too, judging by the overflow from Mee's secret compartment.

A door disguised as a bookcase opened and in stepped Raptor, who loved to make his unconventional entrances.

'Settle down, settle down. Get on with your letters. At least two pages, and in English please, Tavallali and Oberoi.' He repeated this last part week after week, term after term, for he thought it was the only way to teach some of those foreign parents how to speak the Queen's own tongue.

'Gove, are you deaf?' Magnus, he could sense without looking, was standing in the middle of the classroom with his mouth wide open.

'No, sir.'

'What are you waiting for?'

Magnus received a warning look from Bathurst, and was studiously ignored by everyone else.

'They took my tuck, sir.'

'Who did?' This was more a kneejerk response than Raptor giving any real credence to the new boy.

Magnus summoned up his courage. Somebody needed to say something. 'Bathurst and Mee, sir.'

'Is this true, Bathurst?' Raptor slammed shut his dusty old copy of *Greek Synonyms and Antonyms for Advanced Students*, and eyeballed Bathurst.

'No, sir.' Bathurst's face was a picture of wounded innocence.

Seeing Raptor's heart softening, Magnus tried to regain the initiative. 'It's not just me. They took everybody's.'

That was enough to harden Raptor's heart once more. He barrelled out his chest and strode into his role as Inspector Raptor of the Yard.

'Bathurst, Mee, open up your desks.'

Raptor advanced on their desks, forcing Magnus to retreat. The two defendants flipped open their desk lids to reveal perfectly ordered Latin primers and red hardback copies of *Parlez-Vous Français?* covered with men in berets, and women carrying baguettes. Mee's treasure trove was now obscured. Instead, in clear view, sat one packet of Maltesers each, unopened.

'And these are yours?'

'Yes, sir,' they chimed.

'And this is yours, Tavallali?' He was already at Tava's desk, rooting around in the mess and hauling out the half-robbed packet. Important to eliminate others from his inquiries, thought Raptor.

'Yessir,' gulped Tava, swallowing a Malteser whole.

'Half-eaten already, I see,' Raptor pronounced disdainfully. He disliked overweight boys on principle. 'I will not tolerate bullying in my form!' Raptor announced for the whole class to hear and digest. 'Nor will I tolerate false accusations. So, Gove, you will apologize to Bathurst and to Mee. Now get on with your letter.'

Raptor had made his point, and, since there was no more to be said, he bowled out again through his favourite secret door. Magnus slowly walked to his desk.

Mee was the first to initiate what was quickly to become a chorus.

'Sneak, sneak, sneak . . .'

One by one, 3A turned to face him with all the vitriol they could muster. 'Sneak, sneak, sneak . . .!' shouted Goof and Tava and Luerssen and Burkhart, and particularly Bathurst, now smiling triumphantly at his courtroom victory.

Magnus's eyes welled with tears for the very first time. He had promised himself that he wouldn't show his unhappiness in front of the others. Father had told him that a gentleman should cry if he felt moved by pain or love, but never in public. And the 3A form room, with eleven pairs of little eyes focused in his direction, was about as public as it got in a place where privacy did not feature on the list of amenities.

With swollen eyes and a now-sodden jacket sleeve, Magnus made his way down the back stairs into the underbelly of the building. As the bell announced 'All Out', he found himself fighting against wave after wave of boys of all ages making their way out to the playing fields. But Magnus was determined, and he eventually arrived in the art room, all the way at the back of the building. The place was overflowing with brightly painted animal masks and impressive sets of a wooden boat, in preparation for the end-of-term production of *Noah's Flood*. But Magnus didn't even notice. He picked up a large piece of card and found leftover red paint in a yoghurt pot and got to work.

As soon as the task was accomplished Magnus left the room, being careful to put everything back as he had found it. He went out on to the front drive. It was very windy, and it was quite a job holding on to the large card he had made, but for Magnus there was no turning back. He crouched down low to get under the chain that secured the big iron gates.

And then Magnus walked. And walked. And walked. Through the wood, out into a clearing bursting with bluebells, over a narrow stream and through a field of sunflowers. Magnus knew it was going to be a long way, but he had never realized until today just how far out in the middle of nowhere Dryden Park was. It was a relief when he finally came upon a largish road. Magnus positioned himself strategically so he could be seen from both sides, stuck out one arm with thumb extended, and held high the card with his free hand. For this would indicate to any passing motorist where he expected to be taken: PARIS.

Magnus waited. He was quite prepared for the first few cars to pass without stopping for him, but what he hadn't expected was that not a single car came down the road. Magnus started to wonder if he had found a disused road, or if perhaps a hurricane had felled a tree that prevented people from using it. It really wasn't at all like Paris, where Father was always able to flag down a taxi the moment they stepped out into the street. Still, Magnus thought, a car would surely come soon and take him to that wonderfully taxi-rich city, and, more importantly, back to Father.

As darkness fell, Magnus began to feel scared. What if no one came? Would he have to go back to Dryden? Then, as this horrible thought arose, he heard it. It was a diesel engine, and it sounded old, but Magnus was sure this would not be a problem. The black car slowly squeaked to a halt, and the passenger door opened slightly. A reunion with Father was now in sight. As Magnus pulled eagerly on the passenger-door handle, the interior light came on, spotlighting the driver.

'You are the most inconsiderate boy, Gove. The whole school has been looking for you. Now get in.' Raptor's face didn't show worry or sympathy or relief that Magnus was alive. His expression was one of pure rage. Magnus had never seen anyone look like that, least of all at him. And Raptor had not asked what he was doing, or where he was going. The absolute finality of Raptor's command somehow put Magnus off trying to explain that he didn't like it at Dryden and that he wanted to go back to Paris. So he just got into the car, and let Raptor drive him away, leaving the placard, smudged and disintegrated, in the mud.

6

You're Not the Only One

All in all this boy was nothing but trouble, Raptor thought to himself as he drove. Bad at Latin, no good at cricket and barely here a week and already he had made a dash for it. They were in serious danger of a complete collapse of the disciplinary infrastructure at Dryden. Ever since the idiots on the Board of Governors decided to promote that wretched man to Headmaster over him, the school had been on a precipitous decline. Still, if he could get 3A into really good fighting shape, there was a better than good possibility that he, with thirty-eight years of service to Dryden, would be asked to replace the Headmaster. Then Dryden Park would churn out boys ready to win wars and run the empire once again.

And this pathetic Gove was threatening to spoil it all. As he drove through the gates and brought the car to a halt outside the front door, Raptor decided that it was time for him to begin the process of rebuilding Dryden Park to its rightful position.

'Major!' It was the Bursar bellowing into the darkness, standing at the top of the steps, and looking, for reasons known only to him, through a pair of binoculars. Raptor sighed. It was people like that that gave the army a bad name. But he had been the Headmaster's best man, and consequently wielded not inconsiderable power within the school. No matter, thought Raptor. When the Headmaster goes, the Bursar will go too.

'What can I do for you, Bursar?' inquired Raptor, putting on the smile he usually reserved for greeting parents.

'Ah, ML. Not you, old boy, just looking for the old canus. I see you've found the AWOL lad. J good show. HM wanted to see you, I think. He was in the HMS last time I saw him. With a VP. Now Major? Major!'

Raptor carried on smiling but fumed gently inside. Why couldn't the bloody man talk like the rest of the world? But he hadn't been completely useless. If the Headmaster was in the Headmaster's study with a visiting parent, Raptor could begin his plan immediately. As the storm clouds began to gather in the night sky, Raptor led Magnus into the building.

Coming back into the great hallway, Magnus was overcome by a sense of impending doom. Raptor had said nothing to him during the whole journey back, but Magnus had felt the intense distaste that Raptor had for him. And now with the Headmaster on the case as well, Dryden looked an even gloomier place than the one from which Magnus had run away.

They arrived in the 3A classroom, and Raptor shut the door behind him just as the first thunderclap rang out outside. Magnus stood by a desk and didn't move. The windows were now shuttered, and for all he knew he could be killed in here tonight without anyone finding out. Then this very tall, evil-looking man came upon him, talking in very slow, measured tones.

'Running away is not a solution to anything, Gove. In fact it is downright cowardice. 3A is a model for the whole school, and I will not allow your childish shenanigans to turn me into the laughing stock of Dryden Park.'

Raptor now had one hand on Magnus's shoulder, while the other hand went up, way way up, before beginning its descent. Target: little boy's face. Magnus had never been hit before: Father did not believe in corporal punishment. Not really knowing what to do, Magnus closed his eyes as tight as they would go.

'Ah, Major Longfellow.'

After a moment, Magnus tentatively opened one of his eyes. He hadn't felt a blow, and he had just heard a voice that wasn't Raptor's. There, standing with the door open, was the figure of the Headmaster. Magnus saw Raptor quickly bring down his hand, and then he felt himself released.

'Hea . . . Headmaster. I'm happy to report that we have found the boy.'

'Good.' The Headmaster's reply sounded more like a warning. 'Please come in, he's in here.' The Headmaster moved to the side, and a beautiful face appeared in the doorway.

'*Maman!*' Mother, immaculately made up and wearing an outfit more suited to international catwalks, was in the room, Magnus was in her arms and the two masters were out the door.

'Magnus. What's the matter, *chéri*?' she whispered.

'I want to go home.'

'You know you can't. I'm frantically busy, and you father can't even look after himself.'

'How is Papa?' Even bad news was better than no news. At least Father was alive.

'You know he's not well.'

'Why don't we go home together now?'

'Oh, Magnus, this is hard for all of us. Please understand.' Magnus didn't understand at all, but said nothing.

Just as discreetly as he had left, the Headmaster was back.

'How are we doing, Lady Gove?'

Mother wasn't expecting him back so soon, and she almost dropped Magnus as she began to straighten out her clothes before turning to answer the question. Any other ten-year-old might have worried that he had done or said something wrong, but for Magnus, the sudden change came as no surprise. It had always been Father who looked after him; Mother was never particularly affectionate, and was merely a beautiful passing presence.

'Another camomile tea, perhaps?' Client entertainment really was one of the Headmaster's strong points.

'Oh no, thank you. I've got a plane to catch.'

'Going far?' The Headmaster thought of himself as a bit of a jet-setter in his own way.

'No, not really. Just to Los Angeles.'

70

Mother made her way out quickly. Then she was in her car, and the chauffeur had already closed the door and started the engine. The electric window glided open.

'Now, *mon petit*,' Mother seemed much more comfortable now, with the door between them, 'you must be brave. We all must. He is a good man, your Headmaster. You must listen to him. Oh! and this is for you.' She passed over a little bag as a parting gift, and the car sped away.

Magnus was left standing there all alone again. The faintest glimmer of hope which had accompanied Mother's arrival was dead. He looked down at the plastic bag. Nice Côte d'Azur Duty Free. They had a very good selection of Swiss chocolate there. Magnus perked up. Even if he hadn't got back to Paris, a box of Truffes au Champagne from Teuscher was better than nothing. Magnus pulled out the white box with excitement.

'What do you say to us finding ourselves a really nice hot cup of tea, eh?' It was the Headmaster. He had been standing there all this time. Just as well. Tea was also better than nothing. For Mother hadn't got him fresh cream truffles from Teuscher. She hadn't even bought him a tin of stuffed olives. Instead, the box contained a crocodile-skin wallet. Not exactly what Magnus was after.

As the Headmaster led him back inside, neither of them noticed the intense face pushed up against a window high above the drive. The little scene now over, Miss Charlotte went back to work.

*

The wooden floor and dark oak desk in the Headmaster's study were polished to a mirror-like sheen, and the padded double doors prevented boys waiting outside from hearing the punishment being given to the hapless victim within. But in one corner was a very different, and much more friendly, set-up. Two leather armchairs faced each other in front of the fireplace, and a small table sat perched between them.

'How about a low-calorie rice cake?' proffered the Headmaster, thrusting a tray full of such cakes and other health foods at Magnus. It did nothing to lighten Magnus's mood.

'I'm not hungry, thank you,' he lied. After all, rice cakes were hardly food.

'Perhaps you'd prefer . . .' The Headmaster leaned back and opened up a great antique safe behind his chair. He pulled out a small cardboard box. Nestled inside was a not especially exquisite-looking chocolate éclair. But it was the first real food Magnus had seen in weeks! He tucked in. In no time at all, chocolate covered his face, and whipped cream covered every other part of him.

'Fresh from the bakery this afternoon,' the Head-master said. 'I happened to be passing. Not for me, you understand. But we all need a little reward from time to time.' Magnus was sure the Head-master was salivating ever so slightly, but he didn't really care. As long as he, Magnus, was eating an éclair, he didn't mind what the Headmaster said or did.

'You see, although this will never be home, we

are a family. Oh yes. But you have to earn your place though. Make friends, earn their trust, one by one if need be.' The Headmaster was used to giving these chats, but with Magnus concentrating so intently on his cake, he was worried that he might not be getting through. A new approach was required.

'How's the éclair?'

'Jolly good, thank you, sir.'

'You know, I always think that the unsweetened cream brings out the flavour of the chocolate.'

'You sound just like my father, sir.' Magnus was surprised by the Headmaster's comment, but he was also pleased – he had found an ally. Magnus resolved to listen to Mother and do as the Headmaster said. Unlike Raptor, the Headmaster had been kind right from the start. If he was a gourmet as well, perhaps it wasn't always going to be just health foods. Dryden Park was starting to look up.

With his fresh outlook and full stomach, Magnus was more cheerful than he had been since his arrival in England. He didn't notice the relentless hissing of the taps or the aggressive stench as he went into the bathroom to prepare for bed. But he did notice Miss Charlotte cleaning the last of the basins. She came up to him straight away.

'I thought you said your mother wasn't around.' It sounded like an accusation.

'She's not, most of the time.'

'My mum died when I was your age.' Charlotte often blurted things out without thinking. She saw Magnus's face drop, and tried to make amends.

Tugging nervously at her fringe she did her best to comfort him. 'Oh, I'm sorry, I'm sorry. I'm so stupid.'

But Magnus was inconsolable. The thought of Father dying and being left with just Mother was too much. He buried his face in his arms and sobbed.

'Charlotte!'

The boom came from the other end of the room, and it was the unmistakable voice of Raptor. Charlotte turned quickly and saw that he was there, towering over her in his dressing-gown.

'What could possibly have possessed you to believe that these are mine?' His tone was condescending and disbelieving, as he held up a minute pair of stripy underpants. They were so small they fitted into his hand like a glove.

'I'm sorry, Father. I'll sort it out in a minute.' She tried to remain calm, but her fingers leapt up to her fringe as usual.

'I need them now.'

Charlotte couldn't cope. She had hurt the one boy in the school who wasn't mean to her, and now here was her father, who was only ever mean to her. Raptor hurled the tiny Y-fronts down on to the counter and stomped out. Charlotte let out a deep, deep sigh. She looked over to Magnus, who still had his head buried in his arms.

'You're not the only one who wants to run away,' she said.

7

Fitting In

The Headmaster's words of advice were not lost on Magnus, and indeed they were confirmed when the letter arrived. The usual gaggle of third-formers were scrabbling around Raptor like pointy-beaked chicks hoping for a worm. Bathurst had received his statutory letter a week from his mother that was a photocopied form letter sent to all three of her sons. Green Minor got four letters from his grandmother in Pwllheli, whose memory lapses caused her to write the same information over and over, forget she had posted it, and start again. Tavallali lumbered away with a large parcel the size and weight of a small portable colour television.

Magnus waited and waited as Raptor boomed out the lucky names. He was reminded of cricket-team selection. It was always the same. Tava, Goof and Magnus were always the last three standing there on the boundary, while Bathurst and Mee as team captains bickered over who got which handicap. Magnus was the only one left when Raptor reached the end of the stack. But there was one final envelope, slightly crumpled, in his hand. Could it be of the thin blue airmail variety? It could. Might it be stamped with those legionnaires and marked with the seal of Paris? It was. Raptor turned the missive in his hand, holding it up to the

Lidgate's Tarte aux Myrtilles

(serves 4)

For the pastry:
250g unsalted butter
150g icing sugar
4 egg yolks
salt
1 tsp baking powder
500g plain flour
1 tbsp water

For the filling:
Thick blackberry jam

1 Beat the unsalted butter until it is soft and smooth, and it lightens in colour.

2 Add the icing sugar and egg yolks, and a pinch of salt and the baking powder, and mix well.

3 Slowly add the flour by sifting it into the egg mixture and rubbing it together using your fingers.

4 When the dough is evenly grainy, add the water, and press it all together in your hands.

5 Place the dough on a floured surface and knead well for 1 minute.

6   Wrap the dough in clingfilm and chill for 4 hours or, better, overnight.

7   Preheat the oven to 190°C.

8   Use ¾ of the dough and roll out as the pastry base so that it hangs over the edge of your pie tin.

9   Spoon the jam into the pie.

10 Roll out the remaining dough and cover the pie with it.

11 Press the edges together with your fingers, removing any extra dough as you go. Cut a few slashes in the top, and a hole in the centre.

12 Bake for 45 minutes.

<u>Lidgate's tips:</u> Use a thick jam made with whole fruits, as jellies or thin conserves will run out of the pie.

If when you roll out the pastry you make a few holes, you don't have to start again. Just patch over the holes with some of the extra dough, rolled to the same thickness.

light as if it were a forged £20 note, scrutinizing it through narrowed eyes. Magnus held his breath. Was he going to confiscate it? Surely there was no problem?

'. . . and the last one. The last one is for you, Gove.' Down came the letter from on high into Magnus's waiting hands, and off he ran to the relative sanctuary of his bed for a quiet read. With a mixture of trepidation and anticipation, he started to open the aerogramme. Magnus very carefully peeled back the gummed edge to reveal the delicate handwriting that threw him back immediately into those warm Spring days in the apartment drawing room, watching Father writing letters to *The Times* of London, lamenting the decline of Britain. And here was Magnus reading his first letter from that great pen Father called Excalibur.

My Dear Boy

I can't tell you what a delight it was to receive your eagerly awaited letter. But oh, what horror to learn of your bumpy landing at the old place. If it is any consolation, I, too, was not an immediate success. While our respective institutions keep us apart, we must both practise the art of survival. As T. S. Eliot once wrote, we all put on faces to meet other faces.

So brush your hair, polish your teeth and fix your smile. For this is the face the world will want to court, and love, as I do. I, and Paris, eagerly await the exeat. Until then, I remain, as ever,

your devoted Papa.

P.S. Although we are now deprived of our dinners together, we should not allow our scrap-book to go unattended this week. I therefore enclose one of the very first recipes that Scoffier was kind enough to share with me: Tarte Tatin.

Magnus broke into a big, sad smile. It was two long weeks until the weekend break that prep-school boys still refer to in that moribund language; Latin: *exeat* – he goes out. How was he going to survive another two weeks?

Magnus decided that the best he could do was try his very hardest to fit in. He glued the tarte tatin recipe on to a fresh page of his scrapbook and tucked it back under his pillow, resolving not to think about food any more. He sat in the dining hall and gobbled down celery stew without any fuss. He pored over his Harrison's *Latin Primer*, keeping small and quiet in the corner of the form room while the others watched the Saturday afternoon double-bill of *Universal Soldier* and *The Dam Busters*. The Thursday Test results rose from a pitiful 4/20 to a just substand-ard 8/20. Raptor was never pleased, but it had to be said that his displeasure had lessened.

Magnus even hurled himself, quite literally, into cricket. Although he could still not see any value in boys running between two sets of wooden sticks, he took up his station on the boundary with the utmost seriousness. For hours on end he fixed his eyes on the hazy activities happening a long way away at the crease, poised for the rare occasion when the ball came his way. At those moments, he could never win. After countless grass-staining, knee-skinning misses that brought derisive choruses of 'Mal-co!', he finally connected when the ball dropped through his flailing hands and on to his toe, failing to cross the boundary. It didn't make him any less mal-coordinated, but when they laughed, it felt like they were laughing *with* him and not *at* him.

So Magnus kept smiling back, fixing that toothy grin that Father had counselled. Whoever T. S. Eliot was, thought Magnus, he certainly knew a thing or two. Because when Magnus happily handed over his tuck tariff, Bathurst and Mee gave the sort of nods that suggested all was well and proper in the jungle.

With five days to go before exeat, 3A were put on the French Table, a Dryden tradition. French food was served, and the French language spoken. All was presided over by Monsieur Jourdren, the young French teacher resplendent in his suave mauve suit. The *tricolore* poked out of wholewheat baguettes, which were then dipped into the very thin, organic onion soup. Magnus didn't recognize this version, lacking as it did both the rich, dark colouring and the cheese *croûton* that defined the Soupe à L'Oignon Gratinée that La Coupole did so well.

Monsieur Jourdren thought the same of the insipid food. However, he was in line for a promotion to be head of modern languages, and so made a great show of enjoying every spoonful, to nods of approval from the Headmaster. And each delicate slurp was copied by the biggest Francophile in the school, Miss Charlotte. His every eyebrow movement, or wipe of his mouth, was charted in detail, and repeated exactly. Oh, how elegant she felt, eating onion soup opposite a real Frenchman. The romance of it all! If only he would send a glance in her direction, or toss her a Gallic titbit or two, she would be in heaven.

Magnus feared for her. He had learned that it was not wise to stick one's neck out too far, and hers was certainly craned well forward over her spoon. When her baby-blue cardigan caught on the edge of the table, she was catapulted back, emptying the entire bowl over her lap. This caused her so much distress that the soup in her mouth, which she had bravely managed to stop herself from spitting out, went down the wrong way, and, in a fit of coughing, flew out through her nose into the water jug on the table. The table exploded in laughter. Even the elegant Monsieur Jourdren had to clean off a piece of onion that shot out of his mouth.

Bathurst, naturally, laughed the loudest, and the most menacingly. He simply had to get away from the table, or he was in danger of choking.

'Can I go and get some more water please, sir?' he choked.

'*Non. En français, s'il vous plaît. Alors?*'

'*Puis . . . je . . . aller . . . prendre . . . plus du pain, Monsieur?*' Bathurst's grammar was not impeccable; and he couldn't get his mouth round the words.

'*Non. Ce n'est pas le mot juste. Quelqu'un peut l'aider?*'

Not surprisingly, there was no one foolish enough to take on Bathurst.

'Gove?' Like a heat-seeking missile, he homed in on Magnus. Magnus had been dreading this moment, and was trying to remain as inconspicuous as possible. 'Yes, you. Don't your parents live in Paris?' The whole table waited.

'Yes, but –'

'*En français, s'il vous plaît.*'

Magnus blurted it out as quickly as possible so he could get it over and done with: '*C'est mon père qui habite à Paris, mais nous parlons en anglais chez nous.*' There was a stunned silence. There was no question that Magnus was disgustingly fluent. Monsieur Jourdren raised an eyebrow, impressed.

'That's disgusting. God, Froggie,' the boys muttered. Bathurst gritted his teeth and said nothing. Miss Charlotte peered over her soup-stained glasses with a renewed interest.

Magnus soon realized that keeping a low profile was going to be harder than he had first thought. In fact, the harder he tried to fit in, the more he sensed a strange doom. On this particular occasion, it came appropriately enough after the Thursday Test.

'I am not pleased. I am not at all pleased,' rumbled Raptor from behind his lectern. He pushed his pince-nez to the end of his nose, and continued with more vigour. '3A is supposed to be the fast stream.'

Burkhart started mouthing the words, suggesting

that this was perhaps a speech they had all heard before.

'This was the most appalling Thursday Test I have ever had the misfortune to mark. With one or two exceptions.' This final addition was made only grudgingly, but it was enough to make Mee and Bathurst exchange smug looks.

'Bottom, with 2/20, Oberoi. No surprises there, you lazy creature.' He slammed Oberoi's book on to his desk, causing his compasses to leap up and bury themselves in his arm.

'Eleventh, 5/20, Tavallali.' Raptor was now hurling the books across the room with pinpoint accuracy, skewering each boy with his disgust at their lack of command of the past participles of Latin. Magnus held his breath, preparing to catch his book before it hit him in the face. But Raptor continued through the list, and there was no mention of 'Gove' or of how badly he had done. Oh no, thought Magnus, he's saving me for a special grilling afterwards.

'Fourth equal with 11/20, Pears and Mee –

'You, sir?' the room responded, slightly too well in vision.

'Be quiet!' Raptor had indeed heard that one once too often, and today of all days he was in no mood for light-heartedness.

'Third, Burkhart, 13/20.'

Now Raptor paused and adjusted his gown. He loved the drama. 3A looked alternately at Magnus and Bathurst, like spectators at Wimbledon.

'It's quite close at the top. Gove' – Bathurst let

out a thin hiss of relief – 'and Bathurst. First equal. 17/20.' If Bathurst's face didn't exactly darken, it certainly lost its customary sunniness. With neck muscles stiff as pylons, he turned to look at Magnus, who was now, more than ever, trying to keep a low profile in the corner. Raptor twisted the dagger in the wound. 'Nothing like a spot of healthy competition, eh, Bathurst?'

Magnus's euphoria was short-lived when he was unable to do better than come last in the cross-country run that afternoon. Realizing that sports was one area in which he had no hope of improving, Magnus quietly made his way to the showers. He was always nervous going into the steamy, smelly communal space, with whipping towels, flying soap bars and unabashed older boys with more to be proud of. He felt less timid today, but then, he couldn't hear the conversation that was taking place beyond him.

'Let's just take him out of the game!' sneered Mee. Bathurst was quick to put him back in his place.

'Don't be such an oik. What we need is something a little more . . .'

'Bloody? Violent?' Mee was champing at the bit. Bathurst let out a sigh. Mee was such a yob. Just as well he wasn't the one giving the orders.

'No, sinister. And I have just the thing.' Before he could lay out the strategy, Mee poked him in the ribs, alerting him to Magnus's arrival.

'Sorry about the test, Bathurst. It was just a fluke.' Magnus wasn't sure why he was apologizing, but it seemed the right thing to do.

'After all that swotting, you deserved it.' Bathurst was very nonchalant. 'Listen, Mee and me are going on a raid later. Fancy tagging along?'

Magnus couldn't believe it. Things really were looking up. The exeat was only two days away, Latin and cricket were no longer total mysteries, and, to cap it all, Bathurst was issuing him invitations to participate in a prank, rather than being made the victim of one.

'Gosh, yes, could I?'

Bathurst smiled. Mee nodded. The net was closing in, but Magnus was too excited to see it happening.

That night, Magnus woke to find Bathurst surrounded by a crack team of 3A sporties with their torches lit. Together, they made for the dormitory door, and regrouped in the shadows. The first enemy line was right there. Raptor's rusty cough issued from behind the opaque glass, and his considerable shadow crossed the beam of light pointing out from the door. Like cat-burglars after the world's biggest diamond, the 3A unit stealthily negotiated the piercing beam, Bathurst in command. As sergeant, Mee waved the others through: Pears jumping, Oberoi hopping, and Burkhart scrambling. Then it was Magnus's turn. As he began to cross the line gingerly, the menacing shadow lengthened over him. Magnus froze. Only Mee's quick thinking in pulling him away rescued Magnus before Raptor had a chance to register the shape flitting through his peripheral vision.

The unit continued through the treacherous

darkness, and emerged on to a moss-covered flat roof. By the time Magnus came out into the night chill, the others were all huddled over a glowing skylight, admiring the view in turns.

'PB!' they all chanted.

'Come on, Maggot, come and take a look at this,' beckoned Bathurst. Only the closest of friends were given the honour of a nickname, and Magnus felt appropriately proud as he crouched down and peered through the misty glass. He rubbed the surface with his pyjama sleeve, and his eyes widened at the sight of a pair of pink knees pointing out from a bubble bath. At the far end Miss Charlotte's face floated on the surface covered by a flannel. Magnus knew it was her, because she was still wearing her National Health spectacles over the flannel.

Like any boy of any age in this position, Magnus was filled with glee. He didn't notice Bathurst leading the other peeping Toms away across the roof top, giggling loudly and calling, 'Pwang!' They were so loud, in fact, that for all the noise of the cisterns and running water, Miss Charlotte pulled off her flannel to see what was going on.

And what she saw was Magnus's face pushed up against the skylight, eyes as wide as saucers.

Chaos.

Miss Charlotte screamed a scream of a thousand mothers watching their children being disembowelled by marauding Turks. Her bath water splashed against the skylight like a force-ten gale on a North Sea oil-rig. Magnus opened his mouth, but nothing came out. And then whoosh, he was gone, running back to bed so fast that he had a good chance of turning back time and erasing the whole incident from the annals of history. But for Charlotte it was all too real. She curled herself into a soaking ball and sobbed her heart out.

Back in the dorm Magnus was full of remorse, blaming himself for his actions and worrying about the consequences. The others were still high from their adventure and eager for more, and still Magnus did not see the set-up.

'Do you think she'll sneak?' he inquired, of nobody in particular but hoping for some reassurance.

'No way, she's too wet,' came Bathurst's confident reply. 'Did you see her PB?'

'What's that?'

'Oh, Maggot, what do you think it is? It's so obvious. Pointy Breasts, of course.'

Magnus had to think about that for a moment. The description really wasn't accurate, but best not to disagree. 'Oh, of course.' With that, he sank deeper under his covers, praying that Miss Charlotte hadn't seen him as clearly and vividly as he had her.

But the programme of entertainment was far from over. Mee sat up and cast his radar around the room. He picked up one figure in particular, bobbing up and down under a tartan rug, letting out great snores that confirmed one of those lovely deep sleeps. It was Tavallali doing an impression of a wildebeest taking a nap after a hard day's grazing on the veld.

'Hey, Bathurst, I can hear Tava snoring.' It was not so much a statement as an invitation.

'So can I.' And Bathurst was out of bed and standing over Tava in one movement. Once again, the whole team followed, knowing that lack of participation generally meant being turned into the victim.

'Come on, Maggot,' encouraged Bathurst.

Mee filled up a tooth mug from the basin and dipped Tava's overhanging hand into the cold liquid.

'What do we do now?' inquired Magnus, unsure that all this was really necessary.

'We wait.'

So they waited.

Then it hit Magnus's nose. The unmistakable whiff of urine.

'Pwah! Tava! Pwaaah!' the boys shouted in unison. Goof laughed so much his arms and legs got tangled in each other. Magnus felt waves of nausea rather than laughter and, just as Tava woke up, Bathurst barked another order.

'Lamppost!' This what what Magnus had heard on his first night. And now, Tava was the victim. The iron legs of his bed whipped along the floor, and the whole frame was lifted ninety degrees.

'Cave! Raptor!'

Magnus was concentrating on holding up the heavy bed. The whispered warning passed him by, but the same could not be said of the others, who, in a flash, were back in their beds doing their own impressions of wildebeests resting after a hard day's grazing on the veld. When Raptor turned on the light, Magnus was still holding on to the bed. He contemplated his options. If he was very quick, he could dive through the window on to the gravel sixty feet below. It would mean certain death, but surely that was preferable to whatever Raptor was capable of inflicting.

Magnus jumped out of the way as Raptor made a slow and deliberate advance, his black Oxfords as heavy and all-crushing as the track on a Chieftain tank. Tava's bed was righted in one swoop of the arm. Raptor frowned to see Tava crying, and placed a paternal talon on his bruised forehead.

'It's all right, Tavallali,' he said in a gentle tone Magnus had never heard Raptor use before. It was almost one of sympathy. But there was certainly none of that when he then turned to Magnus.

'You are a cruel little boy, Gove.'

'But sir –' Magnus was going to protest, but thought better of it remembering what happened the last time he sneaked. Anyway, Raptor cut him off with a wave of his hand.

'Two hundred lines. This weekend. Here.'

'But I'm going to see my father for the exeat.' He can't stop me from seeing Father? Not when he was so ill?

'You should have thought of that before.' Raptor's parting salvo was particularly savage, and Magnus could feel the tears starting to well up.

Friday evening saw the Dryden grounds full of Range Rovers and Volvos, while the hallways bustled with excited boys swanking about their parents' cars. Mothers in tight blue corduroys,

fathers in baggy mustard ones, both in Puffas and
Barbours, poured out of the building with their
treasures, pursued by the Headmaster and his not
very subtle hints for donations to the sports hall
and amphitheatre complex. There was some hugging
and kissing by the mothers, but the fathers generally
just nodded. Happy families all, ready for two nights
of soft pillows, privacy and home-cooked food.

Magnus watched from the dormitory window,
dreaming of Father's warm embrace. And just when
he felt he had reached his all-time low, it got worse.
Miss Charlotte appeared behind him, laden with a
basket of dirty vests, and built herself up to say
something. Her shoulders shook, her mouth turned
up at the sides and her hair stood on edge. Finally:
'You're just as bad as the rest!' Then she swivelled
on her heels and marched off.

Nobody else wanted to be Magnus's friend either.
He sought out anyone who might still be lurking in
the school for the weekend, and found just two:
Tava and Goof.

Tava he discovered in the art room, painting an
intricate life-size mural of a gold-trimmed Mercedes
Benz 500SEC.

'That's amazing,' Magnus said. 'Sorry about the
prank. Pax?' Without a word, without even turning
around, Tava shifted his width across the wall where
he was working and blocked Magnus's view.

Nor was he welcome in Goof's universe of Mozart.
Magnus unearthed him in the ornately gilded
eighteenth-century music room. For Goof, the room
was the Albert Hall. The fluent movement of his

fingers revealed a young maestro in his element. Magnus crept closer to the piano, drawing courage from the music as if it were a beacon to lead him. But as soon as he reached Goof's shoulder, the lid came pounding down over the keys, and Goof went indignantly red.

'God, that's really ace!' exclaimed Magnus.

'You're just saying that,' Goof shot back.

'No I'm not. You're a wizz.'

'I can't play when there are people around. I know they're laughing at me.'

'Well, I'm not.' Magnus put on his sincere face and edged a little closer. 'Hey, when are your parents coming?'

'They're not.' Goof wondered if he should reveal his secret to Magnus, but realized it was too good a story not to tell. 'My dad's away on a really important mission. He's gone to Hong Kong.'

'Wow. Is he a secret agent?'

'Sort of, yeah,' said Goof, bursting with pride. 'He's an estate agent.'

'Oh.' He decided to change the subject. 'What about Tava?'

'His dad sells tanks and missiles. They never come.' End of story.

Magnus had never seen Tava or Goof care about anything before, and yet here they were, each indulging in his solitary fantasies. But for whom? For themselves? Magnus could not argue with that, but he thought it a shame for them not to share their gifts with the rest of the world, as Father did his love of food.

Magnus, of course, had one true ally. And he manifested himself as an aerogramme, making the cold lunch of ox-tongue salad infinitely more palatable.

My Dear Boy,

I am devastated by the news that you will not be coming to visit this weekend. I was very much hoping that, with your help, we might have been able to enjoy a little feast. A particularly charming mademoiselle here was good enough to smuggle in some petits fours with my medication. Alas, without company they are merely sustenance. Never underestimate the value of your allies, for allegiance is hard won, but all too easily lost . . .

Magnus looked up from the letter to see Tava and Goof sitting at a separate table, picking grimly at their salads and dreaming of happier times.

'What I'd really like right now,' mused Tava enthusiastically, 'is a double chocolate fudge ice-cream. With raspberry sauce. And four Flakes.'

'And whipped cream, and nuts,' Goof continued, his glasses steaming up. 'And a cherry on top. My mum always puts a cherry on top.'

And suddenly, Magnus saw the future. It was all so clear to him sitting there, watching the two starving men lost in a food desert. There was a common bond between them all. An oasis of food: tasty, sweet, fattening, yummy things that were not to be found in this empty tuck box of an institution. Magnus had tried fitting in to this curious world, with a complete lack of success. So what else could he do? He could try to make the world fit in with him. Yes. That was it.

He would make the world fit in with him.

8

The Scoffers

Miss Plunder had enjoyed a quiet day. Unlike the days on which exeat finished, when boys came back with new clothes to be labelled, money to be collected for safekeeping and tuck to be confiscated, the run-ups to the weekend breaks were always easy. For the first time since she arrived at Dryden twenty-five years ago, Miss Plunder was spending this exeat at the school. On every other exeat she had endured the Bursar's incessant and incomprehensible conversation and Major's slobbering in exchange for a lift down to Great Dumpton station, where she took the 6:45 to Stevenage, to go and stay with her sister. But her brother-in-law had died earlier that year, and Miss Plunder's sister had suddenly become the merriest widow in the world. The proceeds from his life-insurance policy had paid for a round-the-world cruise. Well, it was on a merchant-navy ship, and she would have to help in the galley, but still, she was going all the way around the world.

Miss Plunder sighed as she looked towards the school gates. She envied her sister, but then, she had had to put up with that weasel of a man for forty-five years. A little holiday was the least she deserved. But now, not so young, Miss Plunder was still free and still single, and it was gradually dawning on her that she would be dedicating the rest of her life to Dryden Park. When she first arrived, twenty years of age and about as many stone, she had had great dreams of running off with one of the dashing young masters, but one by one they married the other matrons and left to take up headmasterships at other institutions, until she was the only one left, literally on the laundry-room shelf, endlessly sorting through little boys' underwear.

Now she was determined to enjoy herself, and had spent the morning in the local village, stocking up with a few provisions for the weekend. Every shopkeeper had asked her what the occasion was as she went up to pay for enough food for a couple of dinner parties for six. And every shopkeeper had assumed she was joking when she said it was all for her. She didn't care for the Headmaster's health-food regime, and had nothing but contempt for the fruity young lad that called himself a chef. His gravies were too thin, his vegetables were too hard, and there was never enough salt. The exeat was a welcome opportunity for Miss Plunder to indulge in some proper food.

With the last of the parents just about to leave, and having fielded the usual complaints from Lady Horton-Ffolkes about little Sebastian's nits and verrucas, Miss Plunder settled in for a quiet evening's cooking. Her little bedsit, a chintzy oasis of comfort away from the terrors of Dryden, had been Miss Plunder's only home for three decades, and had the clutter to prove it. But in one corner she had set up a neat kitchenette, and pride of place was given over to a second-hand Baby Belling she had bought off the Bursar. Although she never got to cook much, she was quite an expert, and the menu she had put together for tonight was, in her mind, the very best of British cooking. Now the little hob was a hive of activity. Two pots steamed away, and sweet smells emanated from the oven. She opened up one of the pots and gave the stew a stir. Hmmm, nice and thick: half a bag of flour had made sure of that. And in went the final flourish – some big, heavy dumplings, made with white flour and suet (not butter which some people these days used as a cheat).

Miss Plunder checked her watch. The cabbage and the stew had been on for about an hour. Good, she thought. Everything will be ready in another forty-five minutes. Just in time. She put an old choral symphony on to her gramophone – the only thing she had inherited from her mother – and sat down for a little rest.

'There might be some in the kitchen?' Magnus piped up from across the dining hall. Where else would they look? This was going to be the first step in the Magnusization of Dryden. Or at least of 3A. Well, even just Tava and Goof would be a start.

'What?' said Tava dismissively.

'Ice-cream – in the kitchen.' Granted, there probably wouldn't be any double chocolate fudge, but it was worth a try.

'Likely.' Tava's brand of sarcasm was prep-school perfect.

At that moment Raptor bounded in, looking

very smart. Usually dapper, today he was positively the MDMIWWW (most dapper man in the whole wide world). He brushed down his immaculate blue blazer and straightened his already dead-straight regimental tie. He cleared his throat.

'How are you boys getting along?'

'Fine, thank you, sir,' the trio chimed in a chorus.

'Has er . . . (cough, splutter) Miss Plunder been through here?'

'Don't think so, sir.'

'Right.' Even Raptor shuffled now. But he couldn't possibly leave without some parting volley. Sure enough, 'I trust those lines are coming along, Gove.'

As he disappeared down the corridor, Magnus realized that, for the first time, Raptor had done him a favour. His interrogation had caused the hitherto unaligned three boys to defend themselves as one. There is nothing like friendship formed in the face of adversity. It wasn't much of a bond, but it was a step. Magnus built on it.

'Let's go and look.'

'What?' Tava was not the sort of person who passed the salt on the first request, and he looked suspiciously at Magnus and his cajoling.

'Ice-cream – in the kitchen,' Magnus repeated.

'There isn't any ice-cream for miles.'

Tava's gloom did nothing to dampen Magnus's enthusiasm. 'How do you know? Let's go and look.'

Goof threw up his hands. 'No, no, no, no, no boys allowed in the kitchen.'

Another abrupt conclusion to the debate.

*

Headmaster's Chocolate Eclairs

(Makes 12 small éclairs)

For the pastry:
115g self-raising flour
½ tbsp granulated sugar
salt
175 ml milk
85g butter
4 eggs

For the filling and icing:
600ml double cream
300ml dark chocolate

1 Preheat the oven to 200°C. Grease a baking tray.

2 Sift together the flour, sugar and a pinch of salt.

3 In a heavy saucepan bring the milk to the boil, stirring in the butter.

4 Remove from the heat. Add the flour mixture to the milk in one fell swoop, stirring quickly with a wooden spoon. The mixture will be rough at first but will suddenly become very smooth. When it does, stir very fast. After about 2 minutes, the paste will stop clinging to the spoon.

5 Add the eggs one at a time, beating vigorously all the time.

6 With a spoon, place thick, 3-inch lines of the paste on to the baking tray (If you use a

pastry bag, make sure there is no air inside before you squeeze out the paste.) Leave enough room between the lines for the éclairs to double in size.

7 Sprinkle the tray very lightly with water and bake for 10 minutes. Then reduce the temperature to 180°C and bake for a further 25 minutes or until firm.

8 Cool the éclairs away from any draughts.

9 Whip the double cream until it is stiff.

10 Break the chocolate into small pieces and melt, preferably in a double-boiler. (If you don't have a double-boiler, see Father's tip for Poire Belle Hélène.)

Split the éclairs open lengthways with a sharp knife and fill with cream. Gently spoon the chocolate on top and allow it to harden before serving.

Headmaster's tips: The unsweetened cream brings out the flavour of the chocolate.
  Éclairs are quite difficult to make. If Miss Charlotte hasn't got time to help you, ask another grown-up.

Miss Plunder was woken by a sharp tap on the door. She stirred out of her nap. It was eight o'clock exactly.

'Come in.' She straightened out her dress and checked herself quickly in the mirror as the door creaked open.

'Good evening, Miss Plunder.'

'Oh, you're exactly on time, Major Longfellow.'

Miss Plunder hadn't been sure if Raptor would accept her invitation for supper, but there he was, looking even more dapper than usual. She was glad she had had the foresight to put on some make-up before her nap.

'Something smells absolutely divine,' pronounced Raptor, before manoeuvring himself around the small table and the not so small Miss Plunder to take his seat by the window. The table was set for two, and Raptor was slightly uncomfortable being in such close proximity with Miss Plunder, but then, they had known each other for twenty-five years, and whatever it was she was cooking smelt much more appetizing than the cold collation that Chef had left out for him. Miss Plunder busied herself setting down plates and pouring the Blue Nun that she had just popped open. She brought one of the saucepans over to the table and began to serve. If the smell was divine before, it was now irresistible. Raptor rubbed his hands together and smiled a smile so broad that the muscles in his face began to hurt.

'Ah, dumplings! My favourite! How did you know that, Miss Plunder?' This was turning out to be a very promising evening.

'Oh,' blushed Miss Plunder, leaning over the table in all her fullness and dolloping a very generous helping on her guest's plate, 'it's nothing fancy, you understand.'

'Thank goodness for that. I've never been one for those skinny little meals that leave you feeling empty all day.'

'You're right.' Miss Plunder couldn't believe that such a kindred spirit had been so close by all this time. 'I never feel truly filled.'

Some very well boiled potatoes and cabbage, lovingly softened for two hours, completed the picture. Miss Plunder sat down as daintily as a twenty-stone woman can and tucked her napkin into her ample cleavage.

'Perhaps I could propose . . .' Raptor began theatrically. Miss Plunder dropped her fork and looked up. 'A toast. To real food.' If Miss Plunder was disappointed by this conclusion, Raptor didn't notice, as he began to attack this most calorific of feasts with great gusto.

The doors slowly swung open to reveal the school kitchen in all its grandeur. Magnus had thought on his earlier trespass that it was more like a cavernous hospital than an intimate culinary hearth. But without the bustling, frenetic presence of those busty maids and the repetitive Chef, it was more like a hospital that had been closed down. The great room was efficiently fitted with gleaming stainless-steel units: row after row of walk-in fridges and freezers and shelves stocked with orderly jars of colourless beans. Nothing was out of place, nothing was not immaculately clean, and the floor had not seen insect life for decades.

After opening some of the jars and peering inside the humming wastelands of the fridges, Magnus began to feel that Tava's pessimism was well founded. So did Tava and Goof, who were following close behind.

'Told you so. There's no ice-cream in here,' whispered Tava, already looking back towards the swing doors. Three years at Dryden had taught him (a) not to go out of bounds, and (b) if he had to, not to do so for any longer than was necessary.

Magnus convinced the doubting duo to let him have one final look before making their empty-handed getaway. He switched on the light in the larder to be faced by bags of wholewheat flour, wheatgerm, brown rice, brown eggs and powdered milk. Tava and Goof were not impressed.

'Told you so. There's nothing yummy in here. Let's go,' said Tava.

'What about some pancakes?' suggested Magnus casually.

'Where? *Where?* WHERE?'

Ah, ha. He had them hooked. He pointed to the unappetizing flour, eggs and milk. 'Here, here and here.' And before they could object Magnus plucked the ingredients off the shelves and carried them over to the preparation table. Unfortunately, that was as far as he got, being barely able to see over the top.

But you can't hold down the irrepressible ingenuity of small boys with food on their minds. Minutes later all three were standing proudly on top of three milk crates. For now master of all he surveyed, Magnus unhooked a large steel bowl and proceeded to whisk up a crêpe batter. Tava and Goof could do nothing more than watch, occasionally looking to the door for signs of an errant master or two.

Off the counter came the bowl and the milk crates were carried across to the gas hob. Magnus signalled to Tava to reach up for the biggest frying pan. In total silence Tava began to lower it on to the hob just as Magnus turned up the gas.

Whoosh, went the flame, greedily gulping in all the air it could find with its orange reach. Up went the frying pan, clattering against every other steel pan hanging on the rack. Over went Tava, toppling off his crate and landing on the floor underneath a deluge of pans. Goof went berserk, pointing backwards and forwards at the frying pan and then Tava.

'Fire hazard, health hazard. Fire hazard! Health hazard!'

Magnus wasn't particularly afraid of alerting the odd master while in the kitchen, but he was less certain about alerting the nearest town. He placed a firm hand over Goof's mouth, and stopped the pans from clanking. Nobody appeared at the kitchen door. Nobody could be heard running along corridors to apprehend these intruders. They were safe, for now.

The third movement of the choral symphony was now quietly echoing out of the scratchy gramophone.

Outside, the sun had gone down in a golden purple sunset, and the Palladian pillars directly outside Miss Plunder's window were now lit up in all their majesty. Inside, Raptor sat back in his chair, a look of total satisfaction on his face, and a soothing hand on his tummy, hoping he would be able to make some room for pudding in an otherwise full stomach. It was a quiet moment, as Miss Plunder cleared away the big empty plates and busied herself with the final course, without a single little boy to disturb the peace.

Raptor had enjoyed this evening more than any other in, oh, a good few years. Perhaps not since Margaret had died. Things were very different then: Margaret had been the previous Headmaster's secretary, as well as being the most popular member of staff. With her frequent dinners for colleagues and teas for the boys, nothing happened at Dryden without her knowledge. Charlotte had been just a little girl, and Raptor himself had been in line for the top job when the old Head retired. Through fifteen years of marriage they had never once argued, and Raptor had never been angry with her. Until she died. Although he couldn't show it to anyone at the school, Raptor missed Margaret terribly, and since her death he had felt out of touch; he had lost control of Charlotte; and as a single man, albeit a widower, the position of Headmaster was no longer open to him.

But all melancholy thoughts evaporated as Miss Plunder set down the pudding in front of him with a smile an American waitress would have been proud of. Raptor's appetite got a second wind as he took in the full aroma of the platter. On it was the pride of an English kitchen: spotted dick, with the dried fruit glistening in the candlelight, and a sweet steam gently rising off it.

'A spot of honey? Have you any, Miss Plunder?'

'I'll just have a look in my box,' replied Miss Plunder, cursing herself for not thinking of it first. She bent down in the small space to peer into her lower cupboard, and Raptor had to shift in his chair, taken aback, as he found himself cheek to cheek with her ample backside.

'I don't seem to have any, Major Longfellow. Come to think of it, I can't think of the last time I had any . . .' There was a genuine sadness in her voice.

'Oh, no matter, no matter –'

'I'll just go down and fetch some, if you like.' She was eager to please, in every way.

'If it wouldn't be too much trouble. Honey on spotted dick is absolutely splendid.'

Miss Plunder needed no further encouragement. Without another word, she squeezed through the door and was on her way down to the kitchen.

Tava and Goof's eyes widened as they watched the growing pile of crêpes sliding out of Magnus's pan. Up into the air went another perfectly wafer thin, bubbling pancake, and expertly down into the sizzling I Can't Believe It's Not Butter.

Thud.

Tava and Goof heard it. A very faint sound, but

their ears were trained to pick up a fly's haircut at five hundred paces. Magnus, with less attuned sonar, and much more important things to get on with, continued sprinkling lemon juice and brown sugar over the finished crêpes.

Thud.

'Quick, someone's coming. Cave!' squealed Tava, looking from side to side, but not moving much. Goof was in a stupor, transfixed by the ceiling.

'I can't hear anything,' replied Magnus in his most calming tone. These two needed to relax a little. Chill out.

Thuddd!

Magnus heard it. He saw it, too, as ripples broke out in the crêpe batter. Something very sizeable indeed this way cometh. Goof snapped out of his trance, and he lost his calm demeanour. In quite a big way.

'AaaaaHHH! We're all going to be terminated!' bawled Goof.

'I told you we shouldn't be in here!' joined in Tava, as both of them dashed in different directions, found nowhere to hide and rushed back again, crossing in mid-kitchen. If they had been Red Arrows, their smoke trail would have looked quite a mess.

Magnus whipped the frying pan and the crêpe mountain off the counter and headed around the central reservation to the warming cupboards.

'Quick, hide!' he hissed.

'Where? Where?' Tava and Goof hissed back.

Magnus hauled Goof off the floor where he was attempting to make himself Mr Thin And Unnoticeable in the parquet pattern. Tava was trying to squeeze himself into a water jug, which although large as water jugs go, couldn't possible fit a 36-inch waist attached to an already big boy.

'In there! In there!' suggested Magnus with more force this time.

THUDDDDDDD!!!

Miss Plunder was approaching the kitchen door at considerable speed for a ship of her tonnage. With a good wind behind her, and in full sail, she was nothing less than a galleon at ramming speed. The discovery of boys near her secret cache of honey would somewhat dampen her very jolly mood. Boom, boom, boom went the flat-heeled shoes she had kept since her dancing days at Caterham. The flesh of her foot was edging slightly over the rims, but she bore the pain with equanimity. As they say in France, '*Il faut souffrir pour être belle.*' That was her one French phrase and she used it whenever possible.

Boom, she was at the door.

Just as Magnus tucked the final piece of Tava inside the warming cabinet, and pulled the door shut.

But the kitchen doors made no sound. Within the Quink Permanent Black blackness, the three squashed inmates held their breaths. Goof had no choice, with Tava's boot Shaqattacking his mouth. Maybe they couldn't hear the door open. And it sounded as if the booms were moving off elsewhere. Ten seconds passed. No noise. A minute. It was either die of asphyxiation or risk being caught. They risked it, and threw open the door.

The kitchen door swung open. The boys bolted back into the gloom. The footsteps came closer and closer, until they were right in front of the doors. Their shadow blocked out the only shaft of light there was. Tava wanted to sneeze, so Magnus held his nose, Goof his mouth and ears, and Tava was forced to explode internally like a nuclear missile detonated in its silo. His cheeks rippled, but thankfully no sound came out.

CLANG.

Something hard just came thumping down on the cabinet surface above them. Little did they know that it was actually a jar of thick crunchy peanut butter, followed by a plate of thick, sliced white bread. A pair of hands lovingly spread the peanut butter over every millimetre of the white fluffy surface, and crushed it all down with a sandwich top. Leaving behind the knife and plate, but removing the rest of the evidence, the mysterious scooby-doo snacker crept back through the kitchen doors, and paused in the corridor, listening. His itchy fingers could stand it no longer, and up to the mouth went the sandwich, oozing calorific buttery, crunchy heaven from every side. It was the bite of a man who had not eaten in centuries, and the relief it brought would have warmed the heart of any mother.

This was one happy Headmaster. He stepped into his shoes, which he'd left outside the door, and off he squeaked, sufficiently restored to keep up his health-conscious front for a little longer.

Hearing the familiar squeak of the Headmaster's

shoes receding, the boys burst out of the warming cabinet, gasping for breath.

'That was the Headman!' bleated Goof.

'Phew. That was close!' agreed Tava.

'Let's get out of here,' urged Magnus. 'Where's safe?'

'A veritable feast, Miss Plunder. There's nothing like good old-fashioned dumplings. And the spotted dick was a triumphant ending to a truly fine meal.'

Raptor was really full now, and he leant back and lit his briarwood pipe, content for the first time in years.

'I'm sure they weren't up to Mrs Longfellow's standards,' Miss Plunder replied, blushing slightly. The Blue Nun had done its trick, and she felt confident enough to raise the subject of his wife. Raptor looked at her through the blue smoke.

'No, you're too modest.' Raptor never spoke about Margaret to anyone, and wasn't quite sure what to say. He moved on to safer territory: 'Unfortunately, Charlotte was too young to learn from her. And there's precious little I can teach her.'

'Nonsense, Major Longfellow!' Miss Plunder was on a roll now, with the courage and momentum only cheap wine could provide. 'She's most fortunate to have a father like you.' Raptor's expression became serious, and he looked his hostess in the eye.

'That's very kind of you to say so.'

'It's true.'

It was now or never. Miss Plunder rose from her chair, and picked up the tray of Turkish delight as she leant across the table. 'I know that we haven't really talked, in the last twenty-five years, but I've been watching you, Major Longfellow. And you are a most considerate man.'

Raptor was seriously uncomfortable now, with Miss Plunder's face only a few inches away from his. He tried to lean back some more, but this was not a big room. His chair was already straining against the window. His teeth clenched tighter and tighter on his pipe. The delights came closer and closer. The table was pushing into Raptor's legs, as Miss Plunder brought her full weight down on to it. Raptor shifted his leg, and –

CRASH, TINKLE, TINKLE. One whole side of the table fell away, depositing plates, glasses and the Turkish delight on to the floor. It was only Miss Plunder's unusually quick reflexes that prevented her from joining them. The moment was broken. She sat back down very slowly, and began to weep quietly.

'I'm sorry, Major Longfellow . . . I'm so sorry . . .'

Raptor stood bolt upright and dusted icing sugar from his trousers.

'I think I had better go and check on the boys.' And that was that. No thank you for a wonderful evening, no nothing.

The roof looked magnificent in the clear evening sky. A hundred chimneys dotted the horizon like the Manhattan skyline and threw moonshadows over the grey slate, providing a myriad of perfect places to eat pancakes in peace. The boys lay flat on their backs, staring up at the stars, emitting small groans of tummies that had proved smaller than their eyes. Tava balanced the still considerable mound of pancakes on his stomach and toyed with just one more wafer thin . . . He found room for it. Goof couldn't move. His stomach was now distended like a taut drum. He needed a few minutes of inactivity while the pleasurable pain subsided. Magnus glowed with pride. At last he had found his niche.

Two satisfied customers had been reduced to uncharacteristic silence, broken only by a long, deep burp. It had once belonged to Tava.

'Top tuck!' Tava exclaimed.

'Yeah, what else can you make?' asked Goof.

'Oh, lots of things,' said Magnus, who was distracted by the sight of Miss Charlotte at her window, dabbing herself with acne cream.

'Like what?' asked Tava, very keen to know.

'Well, with the stuff in there, we could make . . . biscuits.'

'*Biscuits!*' Tava and Goof became hugely animated, their full tummies suddenly forgotten with the prospect of more goodies.

'They're easy,' nodded Magnus, enjoying this new-found ability to reel in his peers. He wanted this moment to last, up there on the roof with Charlotte not so far away, when Tava's watch let off a piercing beeping tune that sent a family of screech owls flying for cover.

'Cripes! Lights out!' And they were off in a flash, allowing the owls to retake their position.

*

'Ah, there you all are.'

'All here, sir.'

Raptor burst through the dormitory door at 8:45 on the dot, and was mildly surprised to see those three parentless boys from 3A lying silently in their beds, ready and alert for lights out. Most unusual, he would have thought, if he was in the mood for thinking about such things, but as it was he felt the need for a quick conclusion of his duties, and then a curl up with a spot of *Euridice*. That would get him back on track.

'Good. Lights out.'

Out they went, and off he went. As soon as he had definitely gone, the boys threw back their covers to reveal themselves still fully dressed. They exchanged wry grins and started pulling off their sweaters.

'We should do this again,' began Magnus, swiftly moving on to stage two of his plan to capitalize on this small success.

'What?' responded Tava, with his usual searing brilliance.

'Have feasts,' said Magnus.

'It's too risky during term-time,' Tava moaned. 'We'll get caught.'

'Chef'll go bonkers. Out, out, out, out . . .' chimed in Goof.

'We just need to be careful. We could do it after lights out. The three of us.' Magnus kept a steely resolve in the face of the expected resistance. Goof wavered somewhat.

'The secret feasting club. I could be treasurer.'

'You can be whatever you want.'

Then Tava followed. 'I don't care what I am, I just want to scoff.'

'Exactly.' Magnus had them now. 'Scoffing. That's what this is all about. We're Scoffers. What do you reckon?' It all started to fall into place. Scoffier and scoffing. Maybe there was a link. Whatever. This society was clearly meant to be. He looked from Tava to Goof for confirmation, but their faces fell once more, and their feet became very cold.

'I don't know,' said Goof into his vest. 'It's dangerous.'

'Yeah,' said Tava into his pyjama bottoms, which had lost their string, 'it would be another reason for Bathurst to bully us.'

'That's exactly why we should do it,' said Magnus, throwing down his clothes in a theatrical display. He gave it his all. Like Henry V before Agincourt, or one of those Henrys anyway, he stood on the proverbial haycart and roused the hearts and minds of his men. 'We must stick together. We're not in the Colts for rugger and cricket, but we're still a team. We are the Scoffers!'

Tava and Goof looked incredulous, but also impressed by the passion of Magnus's delivery. So Magnus threw out his ace card, and unveiled the rest of the pancakes from under his pillow. Their eyes lit up, their hunger returned and they tucked into seconds with solid determination.

The next day they stole back down to the kitchens and made the biscuits Magnus had promised the night before. Magnus led the way with perfectly ordered rows of biscuit mix in proportioned round shapes. Tava brought greater artistry to his contribution. He devoted himself to one large biscuit in the shape of a Mercedes-Benz 500SEC, taking great pains to carve out the quarter-light windows and every detail of the alloy wheels. Goof just made a mess. Blobs of every conceivable shape and size littered his baking tray, and covered his glasses, face and clothes. You could have baked him and ended up with more biscuits.

Magnus was supportive of both their creations. As he pointed out when the trays emerged from the oven, they all tasted the same. And Magnus was right. They tasted deliciously crumbly and very yummy, and hot, hot, hot, fresh from the baker's paws. The boys opened their nostrils and sucked in the smell. Yup, they thought, 'The Scoffers!'

9

Mission Impossible

Bathurst's exeat had gone the opposite way to the Scoffers'. It had started so well when his dad had picked him up in the brand-new, mega-spec Range Rover, but then it had gone very steadily downhill ever since. Dad had neglected him all weekend, seeming far keener to talk to Richard and Henry about their numerous successes at Eton. Mum had hardly mentioned his colours.

And here he was, on that dreaded drive back to school in the dying Sunday light, suffering from the worst Sunday blues of all time. Dad had wanted to take him back alone to have what he called 'a little chat'. This had transformed into a tirade about the astronomical cost of fees and his grave disappointment in his youngest son's slipping standards.

'It was just a fluke, Dad,' explained Bathurst, hoping to pacify his burly father in his country-gentleman outfit.

'Not according to Major Longfellow, it wasn't,' barked Mr Bathurst in the sort of tone that had made him a legendary figure at Lloyd's. One talk with Black Jack Bathurst, and even the most troublesome of Names would shut up. 'He tells me this Gove boy is going to take your scholarship.'

'It was just one test,' and he came first equal, for God's sake! But this didn't wash with a congenitally cruel man, who was descended himself from school bullies that went as far back as Godwin the Bully, an Anglo-Saxon earl somewhere in the eighth century. (Mr Bathurst regarded the Normans as *nouveau riche*.)

'It had better be. I won't have you letting down the family name at Dryden, after your grandfather, and me, and Richard, and Henry.'

Bathurst had never heard his father rant this way, and it irked him to have fallen, albeit briefly, from favour. He resolved to reinstate himself as top boy in 3A, as school hero, and as top son. All of which could easily be accomplished with the removal, humiliation or utter destruction of one Maggot Gove, ten years one month. He would never see two months at Dryden. That cheered Bathurst. He no longer heard his father on the subject of the Bathursts' domination of Imperial India; he was deep in his own world, plotting.

Bathurst could sense something was not quite right when he sat down at the 3A table for the post-exeat supper, and eyeballed Maggot, Tava and Goof chewing frantically down the far end, smirking. He didn't like the smirking. Not one little bit. Any smirking done around here was to be done by him, and him alone. He mused for a moment. Divide and rule was his usual ploy, but he'd tried that and yet here were the three biggest drop-outs in the form forming a gang. What could this Maggot creature have to offer Tava and Goof to make them so chummy?

The Scoffers were oblivious to Bathurst's inquisitorial glares, so busy were they passing biscuits under the table and then munching them behind shielding hands. Life had certainly taken a northward turn since they had forged their alliance. For it is a truth universally acknowledged that trials and tribulations of the world are best faced on a full stomach.

Which is just as well when a hand falls mysteriously on one's shoulder, as the Headmaster's did on Magnus's.

'Up to no good this weekend, eh, Gove?'

Magnus gulped on the passenger door of Tava's Mercedes biscuit, while Tava and Goof swallowed the windscreen-wipers whole, and immediately threatened to bring them back up.

'Yes, sir. I mean, no, sir. Why, sir?' inquired Magnus. The Headmaster fixed him with that steely gaze reserved for clairvoyants and soothsayers.

'I didn't see you around,' he replied, breaking out into a smile. 'Glad to see you've made some friends, though –'

'Headmaster, Headmaster, Headmaster!'

The Headmaster was cut off in mid-flow. He knew that it could only be one person, and he was right. The white blur of Chef was buzzing around him like a bee trapped in a jar. Magnus had been let off the hook. For now.

'Ah, Chef. Trust you had a happy weekend,' said the Headmaster.

'Absolutely, Headmaster. Until I get back and find that there have been boys in my kitchen. In *my* kitchen!'

The Scoffers visibly shrank into their fennel pâté.

'This is a serious accusation, Chef. Are you quite sure of your facts?'

At which point, Chef whipped out the plate and knife left on the kitchen counter, smeared with peanut butter, and thrust them into the Headmaster's face.

'Look, look, look!'

'Yes, yes,' replied the Headmaster, testily. 'What am I looking for?'

'Evidence, evidence! Peanut butter!' Chef shrieked, inserting the knife into the Headmaster's nostril. 'You don't allow peanut butter. It's too unhealthy. Am I right? Am I right?'

Headmaster recoiled like a snake from a flame, turning his head back to issue a grumpy hiss. 'Absolutely right, Chef. I shall look into it immediately.'

The Scoffers let out great big sighs which turned quickly into guffaws of laughter.

And so the Scoffers as an institution really began. And like any self-respecting institution, it required a swelling membership that would enable the committee to propagate the word to all who would listen. For although small is beautiful, and compact, and neat, the Scoffers, under the firm guidance of Magnus, felt the need to expand. After all, what is the joy of food if not to share it with one's friends?

Tava and Goof, understandably, said, 'What friends?'

And Magnus replied, 'Precisely. In order to make friends, we have to offer them something they want. Something that even Bathurst can't offer.'

So they kept an eye out for new recruits, and found them gloomily handing over their tuck tariff to Bathurst and Mee. Oberoi and Cubitt were, after Tava and Goof, the two least sporty chaps in the school. Their natural habitat was in front of a television. Also, Oberoi always brought up the rear in any academic subject. For him, it was too much effort even to write his name at the top of exam papers. Being heir to one of the largest international hotel fortunes in the world had dampened his industrial hunger somewhat, while Dryden left him with a pit in his stomach that had been empty since the last creamy korma his mother had made him when he was back in Bombay for Christmas. Cubitt was an Irishman with an uncharacteristic inability to hold a conversation. He was possibly the shyest boy in the world.

All in all, Cubitt and Oberoi were perfect candidates for initiation into the Scoffers, and so when Cubitt slunk off the cricket pitch with yet another golden duck to his name he was intrigued to find a little box waiting for him in the pavilion. It was an extraordinarily beautiful box, made of folded white cardboard, and handles of gold that formed the letter 'S'. Written in black italic on the top was his name: *J. R. Cubitt, Esq.*

Tava had spent hours on this meticulous origami, manufacturing packages that would be worthy of Magnus's creations. If he was going to be involved, he wanted to do it properly.

Cubitt peeled open the box to reveal a tightly rolled scroll, which read:

Miss Plunder's
Spotted Dick

(Serves Miss Plunder plus 1,
or 6 normal adults)

115g self-raising flour
115g crumbed stale white bread
115g shredded suet
55g caster sugar
85g currants or sultanas
rind of 1 lemon
salt
200 ml milk

1 Butter a 1-litre pudding basin.
2 Mix all the dry ingredients in a bowl
   and make a well in the centre.
3 Add the milk and make a dough that
   is of a medium dropping consistency.
4 Spoon the mixture into the pudding
   basin.
5 Cover with a sheet of greaseproof
   paper, pleated in the middle to allow

the pudding to rise. Tie it tightly in place with string.

6 Put a large pan of water on to boil and lower the pudding into it. The water should come halfway up the pudding basin.

7 Leave to boil for 2½ hours, adding more boiling water as required.

8 To serve, remove the greaseproof paper and run a knife around the sides of the pudding. Put a dish upside-down over the basin and quickly turn the whole thing over. Serve hot, with custard.

Raptor's tips: The tying and steaming take a lot of experience. If Miss Plunder isn't around, ask another grown-up for help.

Honey on Spotted Dick is truly magnificent.

The Gentlemen of the Scoffers invite

Mr J.R. Cubitt

on Thursday

in the Science Laboratory

9.30 p.m. Feast   R.S.V.P.

Cubitt wrinkled his nose and checked to see that nobody was watching. Then he wolfed down the small pile of biscuits that sat in the bottom of the box.

Goof watched it all through a crack in the pavilion roof, and nodded gleefully to Magnus and Tava, whose uneven shoulders he was standing on. Yes. The Scoffers had hooked their first guest.

To find Oberoi, they went straight to the lavatories, where he could usually be found catching up on the previous day's *Financial Times*, sent on by his father's flagship hotel in Knightsbridge. Although he hated work of any kind, he found it rather therapeutic to watch his family's shareholdings add and subtract by fractions on the pink pages. He gave a low grunt and scrunched up his face to help along the rather more pressing matter. Suddenly a hand flashed under the flimsy partition and popped a Scoffers box on to the toilet roll. Oberoi peered down at this rude intrusion into the most private of moments. He suddenly felt very insecure on his seat.

He emerged from the toilet to face the long line of toilet cubicles standing side by side, some with doors, some with locks, but hardly any with doors and locks. He approached the cubicle from which this parcel had arrived and braced himself. Then with a flying ninja kick he took the door off its hinges, but nobody was there. He looked under the partitions. No sign. How curious, he thought, as he moved off, biting into one of the biscuits. Curious but delicious.

After he had chomped his way past the collective basins full of football boots, the cubicle door on the other side opened. Nobody will ever know how the Scoffers got round the other side, but their secret was safe. They had increased their guest list by one, and their hit rate was a full 100 per cent.

The next part of Magnus's plan met with a lot of resistance from the committee. For the first time since the fledgling enterprise began, Magnus had to invoke his executive privilege and force a 'yes' vote.

Thus the Scoffers found themselves outside the Surgery on Monday afternoon. Ignoring Tava and Goof's last-minute pleas, Magnus went in, passing the red-haired Boggis twins, who had just had their identical forehead cuts, acquired on the hockey pitch, looked at. Inside Miss Charlotte was clearing away the plastic sheets and bloody swabs into the fliptop bin.

'Your treatment's in the evenings. What do you

want?' she asked flatly. Oh dear, thought Magnus. If she was going to be on the offensive, this was going to be quite difficult. He began to wish he had listened to the others, but he was there now, so he persevered.

'I wanted to give you something,' he said, proffering the origami box with the gold 'S' handles.

'What's this?' Miss Charlotte asked suspiciously, holding the box through her plastic gloves. 'Nasty inky ants? Evil spiders? Or something else just as horrid?' And with that, the Scoffers' pride and joy was tossed into the bin. Miss Charlotte turned to look at Magnus, both hands on hips. 'You think I'm really stupid, don't you?'

It's just a temporary setback, thought Magnus, every new venture has a few. Undeterred, the Scoffers moved on to the next item on the agenda: how to find ingredients. Since there clearly was no more potential in the kitchens (or at least nothing except crêpes and biscuits), the only option was to go and buy something from the nearest delicatessen. This was, naturally, much easier said than done, but the Scoffers talked about it at great length anyway. Up in the geography room, the boys pored over Ordnance Survey maps of the area, normally reserved for geography lessons.

'We'll need to get supplies,' stated Magnus in his most colonel-like voice.

'But the village is out of bounds,' protested Tava. He was a master of stating the obvious.

'And it's a forty-minute walk. And we've got the cross-country run this afternoon.' Goof was wringing his hands quite violently now. 'Then we've got double Raptor.'

'And we don't have any money,' added Tava.

These were all fair points, and ones that reinforced the fact that this society had no precedent. But then again, was T. E. Lawrence daunted by the fact that nobody had ever reached Aqaba across the desert? No. And he had certainly surprised the Turks whose guns were facing out to sea. Magnus pondered these great historical truths, and fingered the map before him like any general contemplating his campaign.

'We'll have to sell something,' was his conclusion.

'Like what?' moaned Tava. He was improving, though. He could have said, 'We don't have anything to sell.'

Magnus flashed a look at the ceiling. 'Over there.' Tava and Goof looked up in alarm, and Magnus whipped the 48-function, solar quartz Casio fx330 calculator out of Tava's top pocket.

'No, you can't,' wailed Tava.

'It's for the Scoffers,' implored Magnus.

Tava crumpled into his sweater, then shook it off. 'Oh, OK. I've got four more, anyway.'

The three returned to their mission. It was Goof, of course, who voiced everyone's thoughts. 'But what about the run?'

It was a good question, and one that haunted their every waking moment, and even the sleeping ones during double chemistry. The Headmaster, in white lab coat and plastic goggles, tended to drone. In fact, he had once represented Scotland in the Singular Droning Olympics. (He would have won the gold had it not been for a late-entry taxi-driver from Delhi.)

'So. What is the boiling-point of methanol? Hello?' the Headmaster rapped out.

No answer. 3A basked in the yellow afternoon sunshine that highlighted the dust motes in the air.

'Fifty-five degrees Centigrade, sir,' the Headmaster replied. He adopted a high-pitched voice that was a rather good imitation of Mee, even if he said so himself.

'Yes, you're absolutely right, Mee. Thank you . . .'

The Headmaster thought this a funny joke, and slipped it in as often as he could. Mee shook his head in dismay. Meanwhile, at the back of the lab, completely uninvolved in the events at the front, the Scoffers continued to mull over the problem of how to secure provisions.

'This is never going to work,' whispered Goof.

Magnus leaned forward and opened the window an inch. No one would notice. 'This is how we get in tonight.'

'But how are you going to skive off the run?'

'Just let me think,' said Magnus, putting on his thinking face. It helped.

Tava saw his chance. 'Can I have my calc back, then?'

'No, we can't give up yet.'

The Headmaster droned on. 'Temp's up to fifty now. Once we get up to sixty, we'll have to stop because that's when it becomes alcohol, which, as I'm sure you all know, is very bad for you.'

'Oh, sir . . .' rippled 3A in soporific tones.

Magnus continued to stare out of the window, hoping for inspiration. He noticed a milkfloat toddle into view, and a milkman get off and do whatever it is a milkman does with milk churns. Magnus whipped round.

'Does the milkfloat come every day?'

'Yeah, why?' replied Tava.

'When exactly?' Magnus directed the specific question to Goof, fount of all useless knowledge.

Goof went red, and spoke rather more loudly than he should. 'I don't know everything.'

'Green Minor, do you have something to say about this experiment?'

Oh oh. The Headmaster was pointing a test tube straight at Goof.

'No, sir.'

The Headmaster raised his eyebrows. 'Nothing? Dumbfounded at its magnificence, are we? I see. I see . . .'

Goof realized that some form of answer was required. He racked his brains and came up with what he hoped to be a popular request. 'Could you do the sodium, please, sir?'

'No,' replied the Headmaster. 'What does sodium have to do with fractional distillation?'

3A heard the word 'sodium' and became instantly alert. Chemistry was everybody's favourite subject when it involved explosions.

'Oh, sir! Go on, sir!'

'I said no,' the Headmaster continued, but clearly he was wavering.

'Sodium! Sodium!' they roared in unison, not noticing the glint in the Headmaster's eye as he fished out a lump of cork-like substance from a jar of oil behind the desk.

'I couldn't possibly ... No, I really ...' He hurled the substance into the basin and the whole room seemed to explode and fill with smoke. Boys waved their exercise books around to try and breathe. The Headmaster remained completely still, a ghostly figure in the clouds.

'Now that you're all awake, let us return to the matter at hand.'

As all terrible things must, the dreaded cross-country run finally came to pass. Bathurst bounded up the slippery slope known affectionately as Scratchface, pursued by his hordes, keen to impress. Bringing up the rear, as usual, were the Scoffers, dropping sufficiently far back that they wouldn't be noticed.

For some reason Tava seemed to be particularly broad of girth, even for him. Finally they were moving so slowly that they stopped altogether. In one sudden movement they dived behind a dependable oak. With Goof keeping cave, Tava pulled up his track-suit top to reveal a denim jacket wrapped around his middle, and, more surprisingly, a pair of casual trousers stuck down his track-suit bottoms. Finally, like a magician with endless pockets, he pulled out a gold digital chronometer watch. All of these fashion accessories he dumped unceremoniously in Magnus's arms.

'Remember, you've only got forty-five minutes till double Raptor. I've set the timer for you.' Sure enough, the LED flashed urgently. 45:00, 44:59, 44:58.

Off galloped Magnus. For a boy who had shown little sign of sporting prowess, he moved quickly through the bracken, spurred on, no doubt, by the enticement of food, and the terror of being late for the dreaded double Raptor. But all the while, he heard the words of Father in an extract from his latest encouraging letter.

> During my own sentence at Dryden all those years ago, I spent many an afternoon popping off to Mr Lidgate's in the High Street. I fear he must be long gone by now, but his black-berry jam was a true delight, and I therefore enclose as this week's instalment, Tarte aux Myrtilles.

Magnus reached the back drive fully dressed for his outing. 39:23, 39:22. He peered into the muddy lane hoping to find the milkfloat, but saw nothing. Come on, come on, he urged to himself. With such a precision-timed mission, every element of the plan had to work perfectly if he was to get back to Latin subjunctives with the promised goodies.

And there it was, the electric cart making its stately way back to the village with its consignment of empty skimmed-milk churns. As it hobbled by, dipping into every rut the neglected track had to offer, Magnus sprang from his hiding place and leapt nimbly on to the back. He insinuated himself inside the load and made himself as comfortable as possible for the journey. Phew. He was safe so far: on time, and unnoticed by the driver.

But fate was not on his side. With every bump, the churns shifted a little. Magnus tried desperately to hold on to every one, but there was always one rogue churn wrestling itself from his grasp, intent on hurling itself from the cart. Another bump and off they went, a pair of them, tumbling to the ground with a frightful clatter that a deaf person wearing ear plugs could have heard. As it happens, this particular milkman was not far off that description. A spotty youth sporting his Wolves woolly hat over a pair of headphones, all he could normally hear was the relentless beat of Judas Priest. But he heard the clatter, saw the escaping churns in his side mirror, and slammed on the brakes.

Magnus couldn't believe his bad luck. When the float halted, every churn collapsed on top of him. He couldn't move. Then he heard him coming. The tsst tsst tsst of filtered heavy metal preceded the clump of heavy boots on squelchy mud. Magnus closed his eyes, hoping against hope that, like in the game he had played when he was much younger, if you closed your eyes and couldn't see anybody, they couldn't see you. But he felt the shadow fall over his porthole, and the tsst tsst tsst failed to recede. He was there, not moving. Magnus opened his eyes very slowly, and came face to face with the milkman whose face was set in a rigid scowl of discontent. Magnus hoped this was just how he looked all the time. Tsst, tsst, tsst . . .

'I've 'ad sparrows with broken wings, bust-up badgers. I've even 'ad a deer with a torn winkie, but you're the first of them rich buggers from Dryden Park I've 'ad on my cart. You *are* a cheeky bugger.'

Magnus took this as a compliment and gave his warmest smile. Milky had hauled him up front, and clearly didn't mind the company, so long as the company was a good listener. Which was quite easy because Milky still had Judas Priest playing Hammersmith Palais in his ear, and therefore spoke at considerable volume.

'You wouldn't be trying to run away? You'll get me into all sorts of bother.'

Magnus shook his head vehemently.

'I off-load all my skimmed milk to that tight 'eadmaster of yours. Don't know why he bothers tho'. You're all loaded.'

'I'm not,' interjected Magnus, in the nanosecond during which Milky took a breath.

'Oh, do me a favour.'

'No, really,' Magnus said, pulling out his crocodile-skin wallet and turning it upside down to show its emptiness. 'See? No money.'

'Well, you aren't going to get very far without any cashola, are ya?'

Magnus pulled out Tava's ultra-modern, eminently desirable calculator and waved it enticingly in front of Milky's face.

'I'm going to sell this. Do you want to buy it?'

Milky was not impressed. 'What would I do with that? I do all my sums in m' 'ead.'

Everybody needed a calculator, unless they already had one. Magnus decided that a test was in order. 'What's 28 × 36?'

'1008.' Milky didn't hesitate for a second, and when Magnus checked it on the fx330, he was impressed. Still, it was a temporary setback. Only the second, after Miss Charlotte.

'Mind you,' Milky continued, 'give ya a fiver for that purse thingy of yours. Me mum would like that.'

Aha. He wasn't a totally uninterested buyer after all. But Magnus wasn't going to fall for the old-mother bargaining technique.

'Fifteen. It's worthy fifty.'

Milky let out a bellow of laughter that would not have been out of place at the hippo pools of the Limpopo. 'Fifty! Fifty! Hahahaha . . .'

When Magnus stepped off the milkfloat he held a £10 note in his hand. He let out his own smaller hippo's bray of laughter and looked up at the hand-painted sign above the little village shop: 'D. Lidgate, Purveyor of Fine Foods, Est. 1895.' In the window, another sign, in chalk this time: Local Blackberry Jam.

Magnus checked up and down the street to make sure no one was watching. But then, Magnus was not very familiar with English village life. The word sleepy would not have been inaccurate. Even the local bobby over by the green seemed to be standing fast asleep. This was not a dangerous place. Magnus tightened his jacket belt and headed for Lidgate's. No time to waste. 24:10, 24:09, 24:08.

Clang. The bell announced a customer. A third-generation shopkeeper, Lidgate was a pillar of the community, and it was from this height that he considered the small boy's entrance through the portals of his hallowed emporium. The boy made a beeline for the blackberry jams and started making a small pile of them. He seemed to be in a terrible hurry, and Lidgate was not a man to be hurried.

'You're not a local lad. Are you from Dryden?'

Magnus stopped and blinked furiously. What should he say? If he said yes, he was sunk. No showed he had knowledge of the place. He acted dumb instead. But Lidgate warmed to his line of inquiry and pressed on.

'Does Major Longfellow know you're here?' Magnus blinked some more, and looked away. He felt his guilt was showing through. It was. 'I think I should report you,' said Lidgate, picking up the sort of telephone that Alexander Bell had invented.

Panic. Panic. Be calm. Think. Magnus thought hard. OK, got it. Or at least give it a try.

'*Excusez-moi, Monsieur?*'

Lidgate stopped dialling.

'My . . . English . . . is not so good. *Mon papa* . . . my father . . . waits in the car. We are on 'oliday.'

Lidgate peered out of the window through his owl glasses, and saw nobody resembling a father in a car. He continued dialling the school number, Dumpton 4231. It started to ring.

Help. Say something. Quickly. 19:12, 19:11 . . .

'We 'ave come from Paris to take some of your famous jam.'

Lidgate let it ring, but his armour cracked slightly. 'Oh, really? You've heard of my jam all the way in France?'

Bingo. The man was vain. Magnus nodded, and licked his lips, royally. Lidgate picked up one of the jam jars, and admired his own creation. His naturally modest nature was temporarily overwhelmed, and, just as the school secretary answered the phone, he put the handset back on the cradle.

'Well, it is quite well known, I know. There was an article about me in the *Dumpton Record*, oh, must have been two years ago. But France . . .' On he went, reminiscing about his moments of fame in far-flung places like Suffolk, which he remembered as being very flat. Time slipped away. 12:44, 12:43 . . .

Magnus ducked out of Lidgate's and headed straight for the road where he thrust out his thumb in the hope of a very quick lift. Come on, come on. 10:51, 10:50 . . .

A car came round the village green and headed straight for him. Hooray, might just make it. If this car stops. If the driver's amenable. If he's going in the right direction. That's a lot of ifs to contend with at one time, and every one of them got blown out of the water when Magnus realized that the car was black. And old. With a diesel engine. And in the driving seat, eyes sweeping left to right, absorbing every detail, was Raptor.

Magnus opted for a touch of that old Dunkirk spirit and headed for the beach. Since Dumpton was completely landlocked, he dived behind a large plastic guide dog requesting money for the blind.

Raptor turned and stared at the dog. He could have sworn that he had seen it move, but he was due at double 3A in less than ten minutes, and there was a chance he'd catch Miss Plunder before she left for her afternoon off.

When the last wisps of Raptor's exhaust fumes had trailed away, Magnus emerged. He ran down the road in a blind panic. He'd never get back in time now, not unless there was a miracle. 5:00, 4:59 . . .

Out of nowhere came a noisy red Volkswagen Microbus, populated by a Bavarian couple on a motoring tour of Britain and Norway.

Raptor rumbled up the drive at the precise moment Miss Plunder was leaving the school in her casual tweed suit. Perfect. He took the long way round the drive to his parking spot so that they might engage in some chit-chat. He held this thought right up to the moment when her ample behind filled his field of vision, and then steered away suddenly, resorting to a briefer verbal encounter.

'Good afternoon, Major Longfellow,' she said, allowing herself a coy smile of appreciation for his powerful motor. Raptor was thrown into a spin by such a tender greeting, and as his car trundled by, he followed the line of her herringboned hips. Finally, he spluttered out his reply:

'A very good afternoon to you too, Miss Plun–'

Scrunch! The carefully polished chrome bumper of the Citroën merged with the stone wall that marked the end of the parking space.

*

It was absolute chaos in the bus. Mr and Mrs Bavarian were at least a hundred each and appeared to be carrying their entire worldly belongings in the back. Magnus was crushed in between their not inconsiderable bulks, while they force-fed him liverwurst. He, meanwhile, tried to keep their minds on the road back to school. He also had to insist that his gastronomic preferences did not stretch to German cuisine.

'*Ja freilich, das ist wunderbar, aber ich kann nicht mehr essen,*' he said with his mouth full, jumping out of the van and sprinting off into the bluebell wood that was a shortcut to the back drive: 1:34, 1:33 . . .

He burst out of the wood and lurched down some mossed steps that led through the old stables and into the changing rooms. (Goof had shown him this secret route.)

Raptor was in a very bad mood. Double 3A was going to be no fun at all. Humiliation in front of Miss Plunder and the entire school was not the way to ease oneself into the ablative absolute. Goof and Tava exchanged terrified looks at the sight of Magnus's empty desk, while Raptor pounded through the roll call at an even more acidic pitch than usual.

'Burkhart?'

'Here, sir.'

'Green Minor?'

Goof couldn't bear the pressure. After him came Gove, but if Magnus wasn't there, all hell would break loose. Where on earth was he? He knew the time, he knew the dangers, he had the watch. He'd have to stall somehow. How do you stall a roll call?

'I beg your pardon, sir?'

The room fell definitively silent. It was crazy but it worked. Raptor's elbow fell off his desk. Nobody in forty years had ever meddled with his roll call. Either you're here, or you're in BIG trouble.

'I *beg* your pardon?'

Magnus burst into the changing rooms, bunged the jam into his games kit and pulled on every available article of school uniform hanging in his path. Come on, come on. He was wheezing hard, he needed an asthma shot right now, but he couldn't stop, not when he was so close. He still had the whole length of the school to cover in, in 00:04, 00:03 . . .

'I'm sorry, sir, I thought you called out my name,' Goof contested valiantly, ever aware of the gaping hole at the desk behind him.

'Of course I did! You silly, silly boy,' boomed Raptor, in no mood to play games at any time, and most certainly *not now*. 'Green Minor?'

'Here, sir,' conceded Goof, but amazingly he rose once more. Tava buried his head. 'Very much so, sir. I hope we're doing gerunds today, sir. I'm really looking forward to it, sir.'

'*Be* QUIET!' roared Raptor, shaking every foundation in the building. Goof had done his best. It was time to concede.

'Gove!'

'Here, sir.'

Goof swivelled round in amazement, to find Magnus sitting patiently at his desk. Only when Raptor had moved on did Magnus let out a great big asthmatic sigh, followed by a wink.

10

A Secret Society

The kitchen door squeaked open in the pitch black. The Scoffers stood absolutely still to make sure nobody had heard the noise and was on their way down to investigate. Silence. They were proceeding cautiously, when one of the jam jars fell out of Magnus's bundle and hit the floor like an exploding grenade. The three boys shut their eyes tight, and waited for the worst. But there was still only silence.

In spite of their ever-growing confidence, it had been quite a job to persuade Tava and Goof that their most important feast to date should go ahead as planned. It was term-time now, and it wasn't just errant masters they had to worry about. There was Chef, there were prefects and tonight there was even one of the governors staying as a guest.

But here they all were; the memory of the crêpes and the biscuits was still fresh in their minds, and the description Magnus gave of the tarte aux myrtilles avec Chantilly he was going to make was one that even Monsieur Vaudron would have salivated over. Convinced, Tava and Goof set about assisting Magnus as best they could.

Which was, frankly, fairly badly. In the dim light provided by their torches, Magnus kneaded together the shortcrust pastry and began to roll it out on the polished steel counter. The other two fidgeted nervously, and, as soon as Magnus had finished with the rolling pin, began to fight over it and then with it. As a gladiator, Tava had a clear advantage, and used his height and girth to great effect; but Goof was more agile, and always had control of the weapon. Admittedly, a rolling pin is hardly a sword or a trident, but then again, neither Tava nor Goof was the type to fight to the death.

And anyway, all notions of combat vanished as soon as Magnus popped open the first jar of Mr Lidgate's sweet, gooey blackberry jam. The bottom crust was now moulded and cooled, and the fruit conserve was laid on in big dollops. As Magnus smoothed over the filling with Chef's favourite palette knife, Tava and Goof set about cleaning up the accompanying mess. As in any professional kitchen, Magnus had insisted on cleanliness, and had instructed his assistants to sweep and wipe after him. But for these particular sous-chefs it wasn't so much sweeping and wiping as licking. After the most perfunctory wipe at the mixing bowl and the counter, Tava and Goof focused their attention on the empty jam jars. Now it really became a duel, as the two boys tried to snatch the empty containers from Magnus's hand. Then they licked the insides until the glass actually gleamed.

As Magnus fixed the last piece of the pastry to form the lattice-work pattern that crowned the tarte, he gathered the Scoffers together, grandly displaying the unbaked tarte to Tava and Goof, who fell completely silent when they saw the finished delicacy Magnus had put together, just like that, while they were messing around. They were amazed. But Magnus, proud as he was with his first major solo effort, made sure that the Scoffers all took credit for it as a successful collaboration.

How he would love to have Father see him now. To watch his eyes as he took the first bite, and see them either widen or narrow just a tiny bit, before he gave his pronouncement. Soon, thought Magnus. If he had only had a camera, and if only they weren't in the out-of-bounds kitchen after lights out during term-time, Magnus would have taken a commemorative photo of the three of them with their creation, which, he hoped, would be studied by scholars in years to come as the origin of the Scoffers.

When it came time for the final touch – the cream – Magnus thought that his lieutenants were ready for some responsibility. As Tava's face, fingers and dressing-gown were already covered in jam, the Welsh were drafted in for the delicate assignment. Goof's mastery of the balloon whisk wasn't exactly *cordon bleu*, but it was a brave attempt. While Magnus and Tava took cover behind the sacks of lentils, he swung the instrument wildly. After a few minutes what little Chantilly cream remained in the bowl had been whipped up into sharp peaks. When he proudly held up the bowl for inspection, Magnus and Tava couldn't prevent themselves from breaking up hysterically. A good time was being had by all.

But now, they had a tarte to bake, a kitchen to clean and a feast to organize. So they got on with it.

The Scoffers'

Crème Caramel aux Fraises

(serves 8)

<u>For the caramel:</u>
4 tbsps water
160g caster sugar

<u>For the berry crème:</u>
fresh mint leaves
800 ml milk
12 egg yolks
160g caster sugar
12 strawberries

1 Make the caramel by cooking the water and sugar in a heavy saucepan. Stir constantly until the mixture becomes thick and dark. Pour into a large heatproof flan dish and set aside.

2 Roughly chop the mint leaves and simmer in the milk for 15 minutes.

3 In a bowl, whisk the egg yolks and caster sugar to a light meringue: that is, it makes peaks that stay firm.

4 Strain the mint leaves out of the milk mixture. Add the milk to the meringue and mix this crème well.

5 Cut 11 strawberries into thin slices and add to the crème. Preheat the oven to 180°C.

6 Transfer the berry crème into the flan dish

and cover tightly with aluminium foil so that the foil is touching the whole surface of the berry crème. This will prevent a hard skin from forming.

7   Put the dish in a roasting pan and fill the pan with boiling water from the kettle until the level of the water is ¾ of the way up the dish.

8   Bake for 45 minutes.

9   Take the dish out of the oven and allow to cool. Then refrigerate for 2 hours.

10 Put the dish back in the hot roasting pan bath for about 30 seconds, to warm up the sides. Then loosen the edges with a heated knife and turn out on to a serving platter. Garnish with the remaining strawberry.

Scoffers' tip: If you make this, then you'll have plenty of egg whites ready to make Charlotte's Charlotte aux Poires et au Chocolat! If you don't want to do both at once, egg whites can go in the freezer until you're ready. Don't forget to write on a label how many you've frozen!

With Phase One successfully accomplished the Scoffers climbed silently out through the Italianate Garden to the laboratory window. It was on the top floor of the building, but Magnus had checked beforehand that there was a fire escape handy. Tava was going to mention the fact that boys were not allowed on fire escapes, day or night, when he realized that if they were caught their list of misdemeanours would be so long that one more or less would probably not make any difference. Fully laden with their contraband, the Scoffers began their ascent, suddenly grateful for all those PE lessons spent climbing ladders and ropes. They felt like Milk Tray men; except they knew that their tarte was a whole lot yummier than a measly box of chocolates, and, best of all, they wouldn't have to share it with any horrible girls.

The cavernous laboratory seemed even bigger now, devoid as it was of light, boys and the Headmaster's explosions. Soon a solitary Bunsen burner cast a flickering glow around the room, and the tarte bubbled away above it.

'It's 9:45 and they're still not here. I bet Raptor's caught them. Let's just scoff the lot!' pleaded Tava impatiently. He had a point. The guests had not arrived. The invitations did say 9:30, not 9:30 for 9:45. Goof said nothing, mesmerized by the sight of the warm tarte.

'Five more minutes, OK?' begged Magnus. After all, fifteen minutes was still well within the range of 'fashionably late'. And, as if on cue, there was a great shuffling over by the window. 'Over here!'

whispered Magnus. Two heads popped through the opening, and the bodies tumbled in after them.

'What are we doing?' asked Oberoi, wearing a huge hotel bathrobe stolen from one of his father's rival's hotels. 'Raptor will blow us up if he finds out!' Cubitt showed his nervousness by saying even less than usual. That is, absolutely nothing. But one look at the tarte washed away any lingering doubts that the two new recruits may have had. The feast had begun.

Magnus cut into the tarte with Tava's sixteen-blade Swiss Army knife, and divided it on to five Petri dishes. Goof, still keeping charge of the cream, used a pipette to garnish the servings with not-so-dainty swirls of Chantilly. No sooner had the boys begun to eat than a quiet Irish voice piped up, 'Is there any more?'

The Scoffers all stopped in mid-chew. If it was astonishing that Cubitt had already demolished his generous helping, it was *unbelievable* that he had spoken. But food is a great leveller, and Magnus had seen it time and time again: even the most difficult of guests melted after the first bite. Goof was rather more direct.

'You're so greedy, Cubitt.'

'There's enough seconds for everyone,' Magnus announced with a flourish. And from behind him he produced another perfectly baked tarte aux myrtilles. If Tava and Goof were wondering how and when Magnus had prepared it, they didn't have time to ask.

'Hooray!' they all shouted in unison.

*

'*Shhhhh!*'

Charlotte had only just sat down after her evening shower. She had stopped having baths after the incident with Gove, and she was in the process of dealing with a particularly pussy spot on the tip of her nose which had been bothering her all day. She had spent £6.99 on some New Formula Super-Clearasil, and now that she had some on the end of her finger, she didn't want anything to disturb her. But that was definitely something. Was it coming from the science lab? What was anyone doing there?

She decided to ignore it, and continued prodding at her nose. But there it was again. Even though she hated Dryden and everything about it, Charlotte was conscientious. And so this evening, Miss Plunder's day off, Charlotte put on her mouse-ear slippers and her floral dressing-gown and went off to investigate.

'That was a top idea, Gove. I wasn't going to come, but I'm really glad that I did,' Oberoi said contentedly, his stomach full for the first time since Christmas. There was not a single crumb left on the lab bench as the Scoffers lay back to enjoy the post-feast euphoria.

'It wasn't just me,' Magnus replied through a yawn. 'It was Sukri and Alastair, too.' Magnus didn't like to use surnames, especially among friends, and Tava and Goof were definitely his mates.

'We should tell Bathurst about this,' suggested Cubitt, concluding what for him had been an excessively chatty evening. Alarm bells rang in Magnus's head, but he hid it well.

'Well, we could,' he began, sounding as uninterested as he could, 'but don't you think it would be more fun if we kept it a secret?'

'Yeah, and only Scoffers know other Scoffers,' agreed Tava, glowing at the prospect of knowing something that the school hero didn't.

'How are we going to be able to tell, then?' asked Goof, ever practical.

'We need a signal. Like a secret handshake,' butted in Oberoi. Then, remembering, his eyes lit up. 'My dad has one of those, in his society. It's like this.' And he demonstrated, giving away perhaps the greatest Masonic secret.

But Oberoi need not have worried, since he had started a contest. The Scoffers each put forward their suggestion for a signal, and were now in animated discussion to have their version accepted above the others. Tava's suggestion of nose-picking met with cries of 'That's disgusting', while Goof's adaptation of a Welsh mountain dance his mother had taught him prompted only giggles. Then they hit on it. It wasn't any one person's idea in particular; they all seemed to arrive at it simultaneously. Palm flat, rubbing your tummy in a circular motion. The resolution was passed unanimously. The Scoffers' Salute was born.

'What on earth are you doing?'

A very, very brief moment of silence was followed by mad panic. The Scoffers screamed and scrambled under the benches as Miss Charlotte shone her torch at them from the open window. She was genuinely curious to know what all the strange dancing and tummy rubbing was about, but she was on duty. She needed to enforce some discipline.

'It's no good hiding. Come out of there now,' shouted Charlotte in her most authoritative voice. The response was sluggish. She tried again. 'I said, come out *now*!' This time the boys began to get up. 'And turn that thing off. You could have burnt the whole school down!' Oberoi turned off the gas. That was more like it. Satisfied, Charlotte led the five boys back to Small Boys and went off to bed.

'We're done for.'

'I knew I shouldn't have come.'

'Thanks a lot, Gove.'

'Bathurst would never have got us into trouble like this.'

Magnus didn't know what to think. How could it have gone so horribly wrong? The evening had been going so well, and OK, they were caught, but they had had the best tarte aux myrtilles ever, hadn't they? He couldn't believe the betrayal. And all because Miss Charlotte hadn't accepted their invitation. Well, there was only one thing for it.

'OK. Listen. I'm going to go and talk to her,' said Magnus as the five of them reached the door to Small Boys.

'You'll only make it worse,' said Oberoi.

'How much worse can it get?'

The four Scoffers couldn't argue with that.

*

All in all the disturbance in the lab had been a real bore. Tuesdays were *Bergerac* nights for Miss Charlotte, and all week she had been looking forward to a quiet evening with John Nettles. Jersey wasn't France, but *'Allo 'Allo* was only on on Saturdays. She had bought some nuts and yoghurt-covered raisins to eat during the show (she'd read that vegetable proteins were good for the complexion), but now that she had missed the beginning, there was no point. She picked up last week's *Hello!* magazine and began re-reading the story about Princess Stephanie's new baby. At least she could still enjoy the nuts and raisins in peace.

Knock knock.

Charlotte couldn't believe it. What could it possibly be this time? She quickly brushed her snack items under the duvet.

'Come in.'

It was Gove. She was really irritated now.

'What is it? I thought I told you to go back to bed. My fa– Major Longfellow will want to see you all in the morning.'

'I know you've got to tell him,' started Magnus quietly. In the corridor, he had decided on a gently-gently approach.

'I will.'

'You should.'

Charlotte could feel a migraine coming on. What was this boy on about? She was going to tell her father, and that was that, but if he thought that she thought that she should . . .

'I don't understand,' she blurted out honestly, 'anyway, there's no point in explaining it to me.'

'No, I want to. Do you really think we were doing anything wrong?'

Oh no. She really didn't need this. 'Ask Major Longfellow.'

'I'm going to. But what do you think? Lighting the Bunsen burner. That was stupid. But apart from that, we weren't doing any harm.'

'Well, what were you doing, then?' Charlotte gave in.

'Eating,' Magnus said with his serious face.

'Eating what?'

'A blackberry tart. With whipped cream on the side.'

Charlotte was running out of patience. 'A blackberry tart, with whipped cream on the side. And I suppose you just baked that up in the kitchen, did you?'

'Well, yes.' Magnus reached for a yoghurt-covered raisin sitting on top of the duvet.

Charlotte started to shake. *'Go away and leave me alone! I'm not stupid. OK?'*

Magnus slunk out of Miss Charlotte's room. That wasn't exactly the response he had been hoping for. He really wanted to be able to return triumphantly to Small Boys and announce a peace accord. Instead, all he could say was, 'I don't think she was very pleased.'

'Raptor's going to kill us, Raptor's going to kill us!' came the gloomy chorus from the darkness. Magnus slid into bed as unobtrusively as he could. It was all his fault. He had to make amends, somehow.

In the far corner, trying to read Maggot's mind, was Bathurst. He was intrigued by this latest turn of events, and couldn't get to sleep.

Bathurst wasn't the only one with a touch of insomnia that night. After shouting at Magnus, Charlotte had been exhausted, and turned out the light. It was quiet. Even the incessant nightingales were taking the night off. And yet Charlotte just couldn't get comfortable. She tossed, she turned, she tried reading one of her father's textbooks, which usually sent her right off.

But something was niggling at her. It was Magnus. He really did seem different from the others. He had a kindness, and a sincerity, that she had never seen at Dryden before. And if she was right, why would he make up a story about a blackberry tart? And in the lab, of all places? What had been in that pretty little box he had given her?

These, and other questions, simply could not wait till the same day, same time, same channel, next week. Or even tomorrow. Charlotte got up, and, putting on her dressing-gown and slippers again, went out to investigate for the second time in one night.

Charlotte didn't like walking through the dark echoing corridors at night all by herself, but she knew that she wouldn't sleep if she didn't get to the bottom of it. Unfortunately, the bin in the Surgery was no help. The rubbish had already been emptied, and there was only a fresh plastic bag.

Disappointed but determined, Charlotte braced herself and went outside to the big dustbins by the stables.

The steel bins were taller than her, and when she tried climbing into one the whole thing toppled over, spilling its contents over her just-washed hair. But this didn't stop her. Nor did the freezing cold. Nor did the smell of rotting tofu. With a fading torch in one hand Charlotte rifled through a week's worth of Dryden's detritus. After finding nothing in the first three bins, her fervour dimmed just a touch, but she did not give up. Then there was a glimmer of hope. She found the blood-stained swabs she had used to clean up the two Boggis wounds. She had to be getting closer.

It still took another two lots of festering rubbish before she finally found it. But she did find it. In the dying beam of her torch, something glimmered. It was the gold handle. She almost cried when she saw it, and snatched the crushed origami box towards her. Inside was the scrolled invitation with its red ribbon, and underneath, miraculously intact, was a biscuit.

In the shape of a heart.

A Good Night's Sleep

Breakfast the next day was less appetizing than ever. Not because it was unsweetened muesli bran drenched in prune juice (the standard Friday menu), but because the proverbial Sword of Damocles well and truly hung over our heroes. The summons would certainly arrive. Its path could not be altered. All they could do was stare at their last meal while they waited for the messenger to bring it.

On this occasion the messenger took the form of the school Chaplain, a lascivious old man who, rumour had it, was a former Spanish Inquisitor. He rolled up to the table and licked his lips before pronouncing their doom:

'Green Minor, Tavallali and Gove. Major Longfellow would like to see you in his study.'

The founding members of the Scoffers gulped. Cubitt and Oberoi shifted away down the table, the pictures of innocence.

Magnus had never before been in Raptor's study. According to Goof and Tava, nobody ever entered the inner sanctum unless it was to receive the gravest of possible punishments. Sure enough, the heavy grey-green walls covered with military memorabilia and shelves of confiscated toys had an air of foreboding. Precious little light entered the room, since Raptor kept the thick maroon curtains half closed.

Magnus suspected that this was to prevent the boys outside from being unnecessarily alarmed by the screams from within. He had heard stories of the slap of flat-heeled slippers, rubber-soled gym shoes and, worst of all, the stinging bite of the cane.

Goof and Tava were sure that these corporal punishments were the cruel imaginings of older boys and their fathers. Masters weren't allowed to beat boys any more. It was the law. The Children's Act of 1992, to be Goofexact. But Magnus was not so confident. Raptor was a law unto himself and, behind those tattered drapes that blocked out the light, he could do exactly as he pleased.

Why didn't Raptor put them out of their misery? Instead he sat in his leather chair scratching his fountain-pen noisily across an exercise book. And what was the Chaplain doing hovering in the corner, his hands knotted behind his rear in vicarious antici-pation? Tava and Goof stared, as if at any moment they would step forward and spill the beans, fall at the mercy of Raptor and explain that it wasn't them, it was all Gove's fault. He'd made them do it.

'I am not pleased.' Raptor had finally spoken, and it wasn't a good start. 'Not at all pleased. And I think you know why.' From the look in Raptor's hooded eyes, he knew everything. He was just going to reveal the full horror of their predicament in his own good time.

'I have been informed, by more than one member of staff, that you three −' Charlotte had told him everything. She had to, Magnus supposed. There was no reason for her to be loyal to the cause.

Magnus sank so deep into his thoughts that he failed to hear the conclusion of Raptor's sentence, but fortunately Raptor repeated himself for the benefit of those not paying attention. 'I said, Mr Gove, that you three are simply not pulling your weight in the games department.'

The games department!

Magnus looked across at Tava and Goof's relieved faces, which instantly turned back to mock respect for Raptor's great speech.

'Tavallali and Green Minor. You have consistently come last or second last in every cross-country run this term. And as for you, Gove, you don't even seem to have finished yesterday's.' Magnus held his face straight for as long as was humanly possible.

'The reputation of 3A is built not only on academic excellence, but also on performance on the sports field. Everybody knows that the Battle of Waterloo was won on the playing fields of Dryden.' Dryden? Magnus could have sworn that Father had quoted that line before, in reference to Eton, but both Raptor and the Chaplain were nodding sagely, so who was he to question their historical accuracy? And anyway, nothing mattered any more. All that did matter was that Charlotte didn't tell. He had been forgiven.

Meawhile, down in 3A, Bathurst was conducting an inquisition of his own. Behind him, chasing a flailing fly across his desk with a rusty compass, was Mee, and before him, sitting very nervously, were Cubitt and Oberoi.

'So, Cubitt.'

Cubitt blanched. Why pick on me?

'What was going on last night?'

'Well . . .' Cubitt looked across at Oberoi, who glared back. 'I think we're in big trouble because . . .'

'Cubitt. It's a secret, remember!' hissed Oberoi through his teeth. Cubitt was weak and needed bolstering. Especially when Mee raised his compass and poked it in his direction.

'What sort of secret?' Mee threatened.

'Oh, I didn't realize,' smiled Bathurst. 'If it's a secret, you shouldn't tell us. In fact, I don't think we should talk to you at all.'

Cubitt panicked at this thought, and even Oberoi wavered. To be sent to Coventry by Bathurst was like taking Trappist vows. There would be simply nobody to talk to.

'It's not really a secret,' stammered Cubitt. Oberoi nodded his approval. 'I mean, there are five of us and –'

Cubitt never finished. He didn't have to because Tava and Goof marched into the form room smiling broadly. As Tava passed he whispered, 'Phew. PB didn't sneak on us!' Cubitt and Oberoi checked that both had heard properly, and then, presenting a united front, they turned back to face Bathurst's purpling scowl. 'Sorry, Bathurst.'

Bathurst smiled thinly, and drew himself up to his full height. This interrogation had not gone according to plan, and now there were too many people about for him to let loose his violence within. He looked around for a vent to his frustration, and with one swift, pinpoint accurate jab, he snatched

Mee's compass and skewered that poor fly, which buzzed momentarily before dying.

As soon as Magnus broke free from Raptor's grasp, and sent Tava and Goof tearing off to stop any information that Cubitt might be leaking to Bathurst, he headed upstairs to find Charlotte. Thanks were most certainly due. He found her in the laundry room surrounded by a myriad of damp, crinkled uniforms that required the attention of her steam iron. Thanks did not need to be expressed out loud. His smile and her nod of acknowledgement said it all. So he sat down on the pile of clothes and passed her pyjama tops and bottoms as requested. For half an hour before classes they worked together in silence, before Magnus brought up the subject of a future feast.

'I don't know. I'll get sacked,' she said, as steam billowed up from a pair of neatly ironed black socks.

'But it would be such fun,' said Magnus with his usual dose of encouragement for those who desperately needed more fun in their lives. 'You hate your job anyway.'

'What makes you say that?'

'It's so obvious.'

'Is it?' It was to Magnus, to Charlotte and to every article of unironed clothing in the laundry room. This was not a woman who had her heart in it. 'No, I couldn't,' she went on. 'You'd all just laugh at me.'

'No, we wouldn't. You'd be our Guest of Honour.'

That sounded good to Charlotte. Nobody had

ever called her that before. A guest to be honoured. She couldn't even remember a birthday party where she had been the focus of attention. Not since her mum had died, anyway. She stopped ironing for a moment and considered this prospect. But then she shook her head. Nice thought, but no.

'That Bathurst would laugh, all right.'

'It's not for people like him,' countered Magnus. He could see she was interested. He had her hooked, he just needed to reel her in. 'Look, it's tomorrow night. 9:30 in the pavilion. *Pleeeaaase* come.'

The first invitation to the second public feast had been extended. And in due course two more members of 3A were issued with biscuits and the venue. But as ever, the feast was not going to add up to much without food, and Magnus really had to rack his brains this time. The best place to do that, as every Englishman knows, is in the bath. In Dryden's case this was a fairly public affair.

'So what have we got left?' inquired Tava from his Captain Matey bubble bath, floating with a perfect replica of an aircraft carrier.

'The tiny bit of cream that you didn't finish off, Sukri,' replied Goof. He had a family of yellow ducks.

'Mmm, so not much then,' worried Tava.

'Well, we can't go into the village again,' said Magnus with authority. 'We'll have to use what we can find here.'

'More pancakes?' they shouted.

'No, it's got to be different every time.'

'Why?'

'Because the Scoffers have proper feasts and they've got to be different, every time.'

Father would never have cooked the same thing twice in such a short period. The art of eating involved both experimentation and variety. Anybody can cook their favourite dishes over and over again. Hmm. Magnus mused over his next menu when, all of a sudden, they were no longer alone in the bathroom. Tava's bubbles started bursting, Goof's ducks fled to the outer rim of their pond and Magnus spotted a great wave of water rushing towards him. Something seismic was heading in their direction, and must not be allowed to hear their plans.

'Dive, dive!' squealed Goof, and all three of them dropped like submarines, holding their noses and their breaths.

But Miss Plunder could not be thrown off the scent by such an obvious ploy. Through the rippling, muddy water her image appeared to all of them, towering mountainously, huge hands lodged on solid hips.

'You can come out by yourselves, or I can come in and get you!'

There were no prizes for the response of any sane human being. They got out. And fast. Laughing as they went.

What larks eh, Pip? Magnus was now on a roll, and wrote to Father to tell him of recent developments. Within days he received a reply from HQ that only served to raise his spirits further.

My Dear Boy,

How wonderful that you are enjoying the society of so many nice friends. I accept with great pleasure your committee's kind nomination as Honorary Chairman of the Scoffers. Scoffier himself would have been tickled pink to put his name to such an enterprise. With God, and the surgeons, permitting, I look forward to chairing one of your meetings in person. Especially if Miss Longfellow is to attend. While her father sounds perfectly ghastly (I have a creeping suspicion that he may even have taught me), she seems a most fragrant ally. In the courtship of a lady, always remember that the way to a woman's heart is through her stomach.

You know, Magnus, the more I write, the more I realize how little I have told you. As I lie here composing my thoughts, I can see from my window a charming café where young couples come to sit under the stars. I can picture you so easily, not so many years from now, out there in the cool breeze with the lady of your choice. And you will be the envy of all your peers.

With this in mind, I humbly enclose a recipe which I trust will aid you in your pursuit.

The recipe was for crème caramel with wild berries, and as it so happened, this was the time of year for wild strawberries to emerge from their thorny slumber. Sent on a berry-finding expedition, with Oberoi keeping cave, Tava's bloodhound nose rooted out delicious little dark red strawbugs on the edge of the First XI cricket ground. To the inquisitive Bursar passing by with Major on their DC (daily constitutional), they were searching for worms for a BP (biology project), but had the Bursar looked closely, he would have noticed Tava tucking into these so-called worms with great glee. It was all Oberoi could do to save some ingredients for the feast. Both of them got horribly stung by the tall nettles that guard these delicacies of nature, but they put on a brave face. Everybody knows that this cooking business is fraught with dangers.

Later that night, back in the kitchens, the five Scoffers were hugely impressed by Tava's haul, and as a reward Magnus let the hunter and gatherer wash and slice the strawberries. Goof was put in charge, as ever, of whipping the cream, which still sprayed lightly across everybody within range, but he was coming under control. Cubitt stirred the caramel mixture while Oberoi greased the pan and kept cave (nobody had ears like Oberoi, although he had a tendency to fall asleep on the job). Magnus mixed the eggs and sugar and oversaw his sous-chefs.

It was a fully working kitchen, and Magnus took great pride in their work. Under his supervision Cubitt poured the nicely caramelized mixture into Oberoi's greased pan, followed by Magnus's egg custard, and Tava floated his precision-sliced strawberries into the crème caramel. Goof stood by waiting for his creamy *pièce de résistance*, but was forced to wait while Tava delicately placed his berries. Oberoi frantically tugged at Magnus's dressing-gown sleeve.

'Is it my turn now?' bleated Goof, ever eager to please.

'Not just yet, Al,' came Magnus's calming reply. Oberoi tugged again, more forcefully, but Magnus didn't want Goof to feel left out. It was clear he was disappointed, so Magnus told Oberoi to wait. Then he told Goof, 'We're saving the best till last.'

Goof liked that. Oberoi, however, *couldn't* wait. He tugged again, almost pulling Magnus's sleeve right off.

'OK,' said Magnus frustrated, 'what is it?'

Oberoi opened his mouth, but the words wouldn't come out. Everybody turned to look. Nobody had ever seen Oberoi, usually a paragon of lazy calm, looking so, well, rigid with terror.

'What *is* it?' Magnus asked encouragingly

Oberoi closed his mouth and tried again. This time, accompanied by a great welling up of bodily function breakdown, it came out:

'Ca-Cave. Rap – Raptor's coming!'

Pan-de-monium!

All hell broke loose. Five Scoffers and their hot pots scattered in all directions, clattering into every stainless-steel surface in the kitchen. Magnus had seen this before with Tava and Goof, and he could not believe how the British Empire could have ever survived for so long. OK, Tava was Persian, but if the Welsh had behaved like this at Rorke's Drift, one Zulu would have been able to take the whole lonely veld ranch. Where was the cool, clear thinking of the officer class that had kept the Men of Harlech posted on the sandbags and dead bodies, loading, firing and reloading until ten thousand Zulu warriors lay slain in the long grass before them? It certainly wasn't here. But maybe ten thousand Zulus would not inspire the same degree of fear that preceded Raptor. With one sweep of his outstretched arms, Magnus turned off the gas, picked up the crème caramel and herded five headless chickens down on to the floor behind the central cooking station. Out of sight from the swing doors, just in time, before . . .

Raptor's face appeared at the porthole and filled the round pane of glass with a thick cloud of smoke. As the wisps cleared, Raptor remained absolutely still, and clicked his pipe back in between his yellowing teeth. He couldn't hear anything now, but he certainly heard a racket before. And it had definitely come from the kitchens.

In one bound he was inside, shoulders hunched, every sense alert, seeing, hearing, smelling everything. Oh yes, his senses never let him down. Five years of battle and forty years of teaching did for his nose what a lifetime of wine-tasting would do for others. But in his case he wasn't in search of a bouquet, but a perpetrator. And here there was clearly more than one, somewhere over there, beyond the cookers.

He prowled as silently as a large man with metal blakeys on his heels can. Click. Click. Step by step, radar sweeping. The clicks grew louder with every

Charlotte's

Charlotte aux Poires et au Chocolat

(Serves 12)

4 ripe pears
2 tsps caster sugar
375g bitter chocolate
6 egg yolks
Poire William liqueur (optional)
15 egg whites
75g caster sugar
sablés (see recipe), langues de chat or
  ladyfinger biscuits
whipped double cream

1 Skin and core the pears. Dice the flesh of
   2 into cubes and slice the other two into
   slivers. Immediately place in a saucepan
   and sprinkle with 2 tsps caster sugar. Add
   enough water to cover and simmer gently
   for 30 minutes or until the pears are
   softened. Drain off any
   syrup Remove the sliced
   pears and keep to one side.

2 Break the chocolate into small
   pieces and melt, preferably in
   a double-boiler. (If you don't

have one, see Father's tip in Poire Belle Hélène).

3 Add the egg yolks to the warm melted chocolate and stir well.

4 Add the diced pears, and Poire William if desired.

5 Beat the egg whites until gentle peaks are formed. Add the remaining caster sugar a little bit at a time and continue whisking briskly until firm peaks form.

6 Add a large spoonful of the meringue to the chocolate mixture and stir well. Fold the rest in quickly.

7 Stand the biscuits of your choice around the sides of a large cake tin that either has a removable base or drop sides. Pour in the chocolate mix.

8 Refrigerate for 3 hours, or until firm.

9 Once the mousse has set remove from the cake tin.

10 Arrange the slivers of pear and whipped cream in a circular pattern on the top.

Charlotte's tip: Always use very fresh eggs and don't try distilling your own Poire William!

pace. Beside Magnus the other four Scoffers were so frightened, he wondered whether they could possibly avoid capture. Cubitt looked as if he might faint at any moment, while Goof might very easily throw up in his bowl. Magnus prayed that Tava hadn't wet his pyjamas. However, there wasn't time to wait.

Raptor headed past the counter and flung open the larder doors at the far end of the kitchen. His instinct had been wrong. There was nothing in there but row upon row of revolting dried beans, the raw materials for so many filthy meals. His mood worsened. Then he heard the clunk of a metallic door and he whipped around. Aha, the door of the warming cabinets was lightly swinging. The obvious hiding place. He had them now, so he took his time, marching slowly towards the warmer, scraping his fingernails across the scoured silver surface, and emptying his pipe noisily above the hiding place. He crouched down, his knees cracking as he descended. In a sudden swoop, he had the doors open and stared into the darkness.

Empty.

Raptor's eyebrows knitted in confusion. He swept his hand around the inside. Three solid metal walls left no possible escape route. Foiled again. Damn. He stood up, and his knees cracked again. He could have sworn that he had heard a noise in the kitchens, but then maybe, just maybe, it was a trick of the building. Old pipes carrying noise from the dormitories. He refused to admit that it might be his mind playing tricks. No, no. He was as sharp as the day he joined battle at Monte Cassino. Still. Most annoying.

He brushed himself down, put his pipe away and, having regained his composure, made for the swing doors. Best push off and get a good night's sleep. Hadn't had one of those in ages, not since his dinner with Miss Plunder. Not that he was affected by her – no – he was just looking forward to seeing her again the next morning. As a friendly member of staff. Nothing strange about that.

He closed the swing doors behind him, and set his shoulders back. A good night's sleep. That was what the doctor ordered. One last look through the porthole. All clear, and off he went. Which was just as well for the five Scoffers, hanging from the pipes above the door like bats, still clutching their crème caramel. It was dripping, and their arms were about to break.

12

Dreams of Reims

Magnus knew that an outside venue was risky until you had got there. Their near-miss that night had been the most terrifying yet, and knowing that Raptor was about made the five Scoffers more cautious than ever.

Outside it was brighter than Checkpoint Charlie at the height of the Cold War. High-output floods lit up the front of the building. On the advice of some very dodgy public-relations consultants, the Headmaster had had them installed some weeks before to boost the image of his Dryden as a leading light in the field of private education. As a result, the plants photosynthesized day and night, and it was rumoured that, along with the Great Wall of China, Dryden was the only man-made object that could be seen by astronauts in space.

Grand as it was, this represented a serious problem for the Scoffers. The pavilion was at the far end of the cricket pitch, and getting there would involve being in the spotlight for a good hundred yards. The general consensus, not surprisingly, was to decide on a new venue. But Magnus was adamant: Father had always taught him to have courage in his own conviction, and, besides, it was too late to tell the other guests. There was only one thing to do: make a dash for it, and hope that they wouldn't be hit by too much enemy fire.

The hundred yards felt more like a hundred miles. They sprinted, and sprinted, and the pavilion stubbornly remained a far-off dot. But they got there, no men down and crème caramel intact.

Inside the small marquee that was the school pavilion, the Scoffers hung up their torches and lanterns and set about clearing a space among the row of Gray Nichols bats and old Slazenger tennis racquets in their presses. Then the small space was filled with the sound of metal on china as the boys wolfed down the smooth egg custard. Clearly Crème Caramel aux Fraises Sauvages was set to become another Magnus Gove signature dish.

But its creator, far from relishing his dish and modestly accepting compliments, was not happy. He looked at his watch again. 9:56. Half an hour was most definitely not within the range of fashion-ably late. From the corner of his eye, Magnus could see Tava eyeing his uneaten portion. Magnus had lost his appetite, and was ready to hand his over to those who needed it more. Then, the canvas wall stirred ever so slightly. Magnus looked up, hoping. But the wall just ruffled a bit more. Outside, the wind was picking up. Magnus kicked himself for allowing his expectations to rise. But then, the wall actually parted, and those National Health glasses popped through. Charlotte was there! Magnus sprang up, his heart pounding harder than during any cross-country run.

'Please come in,' he invited.

'Are you sure it's all right?' asked Charlotte,

uncertain. She may have been unsure, but she sure was radiant. She had removed her matron's overall, and had a tartan shawl draped over her shoulders. The big spot on her nose had miraculously gone down, and just a hint of make-up made the most of her high(ish) cheekbones.

'Scoffers,' Magnus declared to the others, 'a chair for our Guest of Honour!' The six other boys in the room were aghast. They had been concentrating too hard on their food to notice Charlotte's entrance, and now that she was just there, they didn't know what to do. The two new recruits, Williams and Merriman, just sat there with their mouths open, the crème caramel starting to drip on their laps. Goof and Tava were astonished that Magnus had actually gone and invited a member of staff. Oberoi and Cubitt were too lazy and too shy to do or think anything.

But Magnus carried on. He nodded to Tava to hold up the dish while he prepared a serving for Charlotte and passed it to her. 'It's crème caramel with wild strawberries. We hope you like it.'

Charlotte took the first tentative bite ... And they were home and dry. Her 'mmms' were more heartfelt and enthusiastic than any Magnus had heard. Another triumph for the Scoffers. If Magnus had been of a Machiavellian persuasion, now would have been the time to ask favours of people. But he wasn't.

'Seconds, anyone?' offered Magnus.

'Mmmmmm!' came the loud reply.

It was so loud, and the evening had taken such a

jovial turn, that none of them picked up a very different sort of 'mmm' being uttered just outside the pavilion. This was more of an intrigued 'mmm?', and it was altogether quite sinister.

Mee was a big fan of spy stories, and naturally James Bond was his favourite. It should be said, however, that in all those 007 films, it wasn't Bond that Mee identified with. It wasn't even Blofeld or Scaramanga. Mee wanted to be Jaws or Oddjob: silent but deadly. Having completed his secret reconnaissance of what the 3A drop-outs were getting up to after lights out, he scampered back into the night. Musing.

The following morning there was nothing Chef could find amusing. Since the abominable peanut butter incident, he had become more protective than ever about his kitchen. He had urged the installation of locks on all the entrances, but had been told by the Headmaster that this was a school, not a prison. But he was not to be put off. He just had to use some inventiveness.

And so Chef had spent the best part of the previous evening booby-trapping his domain. Wholewheat spaghetti was commissioned to take on a new role as chief of security. Lengths of it were discreetly Sellotaped to various openings in the kitchen: the big swing doors, the warming cabinet, the refrigerator. Any unauthorized entry would then be revealed by broken strands.

And this morning every single one of them had been breached. Broken spaghetti was on the cabinets, fridges and larder. As he picked off the pasta and tape débris from all parts of his kitchen, being careful to wipe off every last bit of residual tape glue, Chef planned his next move. He knew that he wouldn't get any support from the Headmaster, so it was up to him.

Up in the Surgery later on, the mood was far lighter. Magnus had deliberately put himself at the back of the queue so that he would get to linger with Charlotte after his asthma treatment. Horton-Ffolkes's verruca had grown and multiplied, and Magnus had a long wait, but it was worth it when Charlotte pulled out a new postcard, and told him all about her pen-pal.

'She's in Reems. Lucky her,' she continued, examining every detail of the town's cathedral that was shown in the faded photograph. It was the sort of postcard that had remained unsold for several reasons, and was being given away at Agences Postes all over town. But Charlotte didn't mind a bit; it was from France, and for that she was green with envy.

'Reims. It's pronounced Reims. It's where they make champagne.' Father had taken Magnus there two summers ago on the way back from Strasbourg, where they had been to try the new season's foie gras.

'Is it really? What's it like? I've never had champagne.' Charlotte couldn't believe how much Magnus knew. He was half her age, and yet she felt like a little girl when she was with him. She stretched out on the surgery bed, propping her chin up in her palms. She was really enjoying this conversation.

'How should I know? I'm only ten.' They both laughed laughs that only the closest of friends can ever share. Magnus wheeled himself over towards the bed on the wheelchair he was playing on.

'Well, will you take me to Reims, then, for my birthday?' asked Charlotte jokingly. Oh, if only he was just a few years older!

Magnus rose to the challenge and replied in his most grown-up voice, 'Well, if you can get me that chit to get me "Off Games", I'll pop down to the travel agents and see what I can do. When would you like to go?'

'It's a busy month,' Charlotte began, looking over to her Beauty of France calendar. 'First there's the formal ball, then my coming-out dance, and after that I'm away on my round-the-world cruise.' Magnus followed her gaze, and was not altogether surprised to find just one entry: '4B Nit Inspection', on the 22nd.

The mood was suddenly no longer that of men in dinner jackets and ladies in ball gowns sipping cocktails on the deck of the *QE2*. Reality was calling again.

'Oh well, it was a nice thought. I'd better head back to the dorm,' said Magnus gloomily as he got out of the wheelchair. Charlotte was an avid day-dreamer, but Magnus had spotted the other – small – entry: 'Sat. 26th – B-day!!!'

13

Harmony Among the Flock

The next day was one of the highlights of every summer term at Dryden: the Broomstick Match. The staff pitted their very best bowlers and batsmen against the finest cricketers in the school, but in the spirit of fairness, the masters used old bats that had been cut down to the width of a broomstick, so that the boys would not be put at an unfair disadvantage.

So the whole school gathered on the First XI pitch to witness the Davids fighting it out with the Goliaths. As a special incentive, a boys' victory meant that the whole school was granted double tuck, and the omens were good. After three solid weeks of rain, culminating in a spectacular thunderstorm that morning, the skies had cleared. Had the match been rained off, as it had the previous year, double tuck was off too.

The Headmaster, of course, hated these occasions, but he fully appreciated the importance of staging events that introduced equality among the staff and boys. It had been his wife's idea, after a particularly successful Christmas lunch when they had played host to the kitchen maids and cleaners at the school. He had hated that too, but his wife had assured him that humility paid dividends in the long term. And dividends were something he liked very much. The more the better. So there he stood, in his white coat and brand-new trilby, doing his Dickie Bird best.

The masters had won the toss, but under Bathurst's solid captaincy the boys made short shrift of Chef and Mr Crotchet, the music master, who had opened the batting. The masters were now 12 for two, Bursar in to bat.

'M and L, please, HM.'

The Headmaster pointed him to middle and leg, and looked over to check square leg. Umpiring there was the Chaplain, licking his lips and scratching his backside. The Headmaster made a mental note to have a word with him about that – at least he must refrain in public. With a quick pucker of his rubbery lips, the Chaplain signalled he was ready.

They were halfway through his over, and Mee was bowling very competently. He thought he would ease the Bursar in gently, and took only a short run up and bounced a medium speed ball. A light whack, and the ball arced up, heading very nicely towards Oberoi at silly mid-on. But he was no Kapil Dev. The red leather slipped slowly through his fingers, plopping loudly on to his shoe. With a quick grunt the Bursar made it to the other side: 13 for two. Mee couldn't believe it. He began to shout 'Butterfingers', but the Headmaster's glare made him think better of it.

Monsieur Jourdren was at the crease now, his elegant whites counterpointed by a paisley cravat. Mee didn't like him. He was a Frog. And he would be damned if a Frog was going to take any runs off him; his grandpa had been shot in the arse by a Frog when he was liberating Paris. Shouldn't be too hard though, Mee thought. Frogs weren't good at cricket; they weren't much good at anything.

So he took only a slightly longer run up. But he was interrupted in mid-stride when Miss Charlotte cut straight across his path on her bicycle. The players all watched as she made her way gracefully across the pitch. She was in her casual clothes, and she had a shopping bag in her basket. She looked confident and happy, and the whole school was more puzzled by that than by the fact that she had cycled straight through the most important cricket match of the term. The Headmaster was annoyed: he didn't want to be out there any longer than necessary. He signalled play to continue.

But Monsieur Jourdren was still looking. And when Mee's fast ball crashed through the stumps, one of the bails jumped up and hit him in the face. Oooph. '*Owzat?!*'

He gesticulated Frenchly to the Headmaster. '*Mais non!*' he cried. He hadn't been ready.

But the Headmaster saw an opportunity for an early conclusion. He pronounced Monsieur Jourdren out. Burkhart, keeping wicket, let out a great cheer and threw the ball high into the air, catching it cleanly as it came back down.

Monsieur Jourdren returned to the pavilion, huffing much more loudly than a good sport should, and sat down on the bench beside the masters' captain. Victor 'Botham' Longfellow occasionally still played for Dumpton, and today, as ever, his six four frame was attired in blindingly white whites, with perfectly creased trousers and not a grass stain in sight. He was a good cricketer, everybody agreed, but his play was more Boycott than Botham, and he was not a crowd-pleaser. But Raptor had met 'Ian' once, and since then he had modelled his style on him.

But such thoughts were temporarily far from his mind. His stare was fixed on the fast-disappearing Charlotte. Never in his forty years as an educator had he witnessed such disrespectful behaviour. And from his own daughter too! An apology would have to be made in the Staff Common Room later.

'*Dépêche-toi, Victor!*'

Raptor snapped out of his anger. He, team captain, was in at number five. The masters' performance so far had been pitiful, but now he would go out there and restore them to their rightful winning position. As far as Raptor was concerned, double tuck was about as likely as Dryden starting to teach Japanese. But what was Jourdren doing, telling him to get a move on? All in good time, was Raptor's motto. And besides, hadn't Jourdren's score been particularly pathetic? Well he wasn't going to get away with that.

'Out for another *canard*, eh, Valéry?'

'Bloody silly *rosbif* game!' was all Monsieur Jourdren had to say, as he ripped off his gloves and threw his pads to the ground.

Raptor allowed himself a little chuckle and slowly pulled himself up to his full height, taking in two large lungfuls of the fresh scent of mown grass. Miss Plunder put down her knitting and gave him solitary applause. He ambled towards the pitch, swinging his Duncan Fearnley (three springs) bat to gently exercise his arm. No broomstick for him. Raptor didn't believe in handicaps; they were for cowards.

There was absolutely no rush. It was a beautiful day, and chances were he was going to be in the whole afternoon. Once the masters had scored two hundred, the boys had to give them an automatic walk-over. Double tuck, my foot.

Lost in these thoughts of yet another triumph, Raptor didn't hear a Gallic giggle shoot up behind him. Back on the bench Monsieur Jourdren was examining a small plastic bowl. It was moulded in a triangular shape, and it was every cricketer's best friend. Its technical term is a box, its function to protect, the – er – crown jewels. Nothing particularly funny about that. Only this one was clearly marked V.E.L.

As Raptor approached the crease, the fielders sank back. Bathurst was a good strategist as well as an all-rounder, and he knew that for Raptor's innings much of the fielding would be done near the boundary.

'Middle and leg, please, Headmaster,' boomed Raptor. He moved his bat backwards and forwards, making the minutest of adjustments.

'That's exactly where you were before, Major Longfellow,' shouted the Headmaster, wishing the man would just get on with it. Still, he was the only one with a hope of preventing double tuck, and that would save a good £48.50.

'Thank you,' replied Raptor, who proceeded to mark his groove with some panache. The job done, he looked up and around the boundary.

'Sure they're far enough back, Bathurst?' he asked. He would warm them up with a few fours before he started some serious slogging.

Bathurst signalled to his team to go deeper still, with virtually every man now at the boundary. Including Mee, preparing for the longest run up of all time. Raptor's radar spotted him straight away.

Raptor was not impressed. 'Ah, Mee, hope you're feeling quick today.' He pulled down the peak of his Dumpton cap and faced the ball.

Mee dug into the ball over and over with his thumbnail. He loosened his shoulder muscles. The Headmaster's signal came, and he was off, sprinting towards the square. The ball left Mee's hand with a whoosh. A speed camera would have clocked its progress at 105 m.p.h. It flashed quickly towards Raptor, with only the slightest of bounces to slow it down. Raptor raised his bat.

C.R.A.C.K.

A pheasant's lone mating call was the only other sound in the ensuing silence.

Raptor experienced the most excruciating pain that he, or any man, ever could. The usual composure of his expression fell away and was replaced by the face of a human being in the throes of death. Clutching his groin, Raptor fell to the ground. It had been a direct hit. The Headmaster and the spectators covered their mouths in sympathy, while the Chaplain grabbed at his own equipment to protect himself from any other stray balls. Even Mee looked sheepish. The mighty had well and truly fallen.

'Oh, my giddy aunt!' shrieked Miss Plunder from

the sidelines. In one bound she discarded her knitting, picked up the first-aid box, and ran – no, sprinted – to the scene of the crime.

'Oh! Major Longfellow! Whatever made you come out without protection?' Miss Plunder had never been so worried in all her life. The poor man had already lost his wife. The Lord really was unfair if any permanent damage had now been done as well.

'Don't worry, I'll have you up again in no time,' she said soothingly. 'Gather round, boys, gather round. And turn around.' At her command they formed a human shield around the patient to shut out any nosy parkers hoping for a glimpse of something.

The boys forming the shield had been giggling, but as they heard Raptor's trousers being undone and the zip coming down, they fell silent to hear what might come next.

'Oh!' exclaimed Miss Plunder. 'Major Long. Fellow!!!'

At the far end of the Italianate Garden an old fountain spurted to life, water gushing out of the shaft. The three Scoffers had just finished raking out all the dead leaves, as punishment for their poor cross-country performance. As unlikely a setting as this was, a top-level meeting was in progress.

'It's time for another feast. And this one is going to be really ace,' announced Magnus.

'What's it going to be this time?' Goof blurted, unable to wait, as he wiped slimy mud from his glasses.

'The only problem is, we're going to need an awful lot of chocolate.' And with that Magnus unveiled his scrapbook to the viewing public for the very first time. He carefully opened it up and slowly pulled back the thin leaf of parchment paper. And there, in Father's elegant hand, was the recipe: Charlotte aux Poires et au Chocolat. And, just as Magnus had warned, it called for fourteen ounces of pure melting chocolate.

'Why don't we just use less chocolate?' It was more than Tava's jobsworth to worry about details like that.

'No,' Magnus rejected firmly, 'fourteen ounces is what the recipe wants. Fourteen ounces is what she'll get.' Who were they, mere ten-year-old Scoffers, to mess with the *grand maître* Scoffier?

'*No!*' Magnus was adamant. This time his adversary was none other than the grandmaster of 3A. Bathurst was collecting his tuck tariff.

'I beg your pardon?' Bathurst asked, disarmingly polite.

'Hand it over. *Now!*' urged Mee, rather less nicely.

'No.' The three Scoffers were joined by a petrified Cubitt and Oberoi.

'I see. And what about the rest of you?'

'They're not going to pay either.'

Bathurst allowed a menacing pause. Then, 'I don't think I heard you correctly. What makes you think you're so special? I think we need to teach you a lesson.'

Mee got up off his desk and all four feet of him tensed up. Loosening his shoulder muscles, he clenched his fists tight. Magnus closed his eyes and prepared to take the blow. Martyrdom was an occupational hazard for a great leader.

Mee went right up to him, but before his punch could connect Tava threw his entire bulk at the assaulter, sending him down to the floor, skidding across the smooth parquet.

'We're not going to pay,' growled Tava, with real conviction in his voice.

Bathurst prepared to take up the fight himself. But the Lord was looking out for the Scoffers, for at that instant, He felt it fit to send in the cavalry.

'Harmony among the flock, boys,' preached the Chaplain as he came through the door to begin double divinity.

Having successfully defied Bathurst, Magnus felt confident to proceed with the feast to top all feasts. Tava was on board. He'd never felt so happy (illustrated amply by the fact that he hadn't wet his bed in weeks). Goof, on the other hand, was becoming increasingly nervous. Watching Tava preparing yet more invitation boxes convinced him that they were on to too much of a good thing.

'I'm not sure, Magnus, I'm not really sure,' he worried, crumbling a Scoffer biscuit all over himself.

'About what?' asked Magnus, enjoying Tava's attention to the detail.

'It keeps on getting bigger.'

'What's wrong with that?'

'We're going to get caught, I know it.'

'No, we're not.'

'It's all right for you. You hate it here. My dad's going to kill me.'

Magnus realized that Goof was facing a crisis of confidence. It was well known that Goof's dad scraped together every penny he earned from his estate agency business in Swansea to send Goof to Dryden. Magnus sympathized but he couldn't allow Goof to withdraw at this point, nor was it fair to be accused of having nothing to lose himself.

'I don't hate it here,' he said gently. 'This is where my friends are. That's why I want them to have feasts with us.' Magnus gave Goof a warm smile, and Goof returned it weakly. Magnus rubbed his tummy in the Scoffers' salute. 'OK?'

Goof let his mouth turn up into a smile, and rubbed his tummy in return. 'OK.'

Tava looked up at both of them, and wrapped his arms around their shoulders, pulling them both down to witness his new creation on the art table. It was a beautiful illustrated invitation to:

A Feast at Midnight

🌿 POOLSIDE DINING 🌿

They were united again. All for one and one for all.

At lunchtime, over vegetarian bake and out of earshot of the Bathurst/Mee combination, they pressed on with the arrangements.

'There are pears in the orchard, biscuits are easy, and we've got loads of chocolate now. Haven't we, Sukri?'

Tava sulkily handed over his last piece of tuck. He'd hoped that it would not have been missed. 'I just wanted a little bit . . .'

Magnus accepted the Flake with gratitude. He knew how hard it was for Tava to postpone his chocolate intake until the feast.

'We've done really well so far. But there's more to get.'

'What now?' Goof's blood pressure rose again.

'Half a teaspoon of Poire William,' said Magnus, as if this were a perfectly common request.

'What's that?' Cubitt asked what everybody else wanted to know.

'It's a pong,' giggled Tava. 'Pw-ah Williams!'

Williams, who was famous for letting off unsavoury trouser coughs, was not amused.

'It's a liqueur,' Magnus continued, keeping them all on track. 'It's a drink . . . You know, alcohol.'

The 'a'-word had a dramatic effect on the Scoffers. Most of them had never touched a drop of the stuff, not even a swig of wine with dinner. It simply didn't happen in English households until much later, and then they tended to make up for lost time.

Goof's response was one of blind panic. 'Oh no, my dad's going to kill me . . .'

But before he had time to describe in full lurid detail how his ex-miner father was going to separate his limbs from his spindly body, the bell sounded and Raptor stood up.

'The following are to report to Miss Plunder after lunch for weighing: Fenner, Rowley and Tavallali. That will not excuse you from games, Tavallali.'

Magnus saw how hurt Tava was by this public humiliation, and gave him a friendly punch to cheer him up.

Raptor rolled on, oblivious. 'Oh, yes, and I believe Chef has a *few* words to say.'

All eyes turned to Chef, standing in front of his sacred kitchen doors, like the Guard at Buckingham Palace. But unlike those silent soldiers in their bearskins, Chef launched into a shrill tirade.

'Look at this sign. Look, look, look. What does it say? What does it say?' This was clearly a rhetorical question. 'Out of bounds to all boys. And that means all boys. Some person, or persons, has or have been trespassing in my kitchen, *in my kitchen*! And I won't have it. I won't. And I don't want to have to repeat myself. Do I? Do I?' Without waiting for an answer he nipped back inside. Nobody, surely, would defy him now. But outside in the dining hall two hundred boys started to giggle – all except the Scoffers and Miss Charlotte, a fact that didn't go unnoticed by Raptor. Or Bathurst.

He had come to the conclusion that 3A's flagrant abuse of his authority had now gone well beyond a joke. And somebody was going to have to pay. Like many bullies, Bathurst selected the person closest to

Justin's
Flambéed Bananas
(serves 4)

4 ripe bananas
100g unsalted butter
50g caster sugar
125ml dark rum
Tava's and Goof's sablés
  (see recipe), or any plain biscuits
strawberries, raspberries, blueberries
  (or a mixture of any of these)
fresh mint
vanilla ice-cream

1. Peel the bananas and slice in half lengthways.
2. Melt the butter in a large frying pan and stir in the sugar. Cook until the mixture has lightly caramelized.

3. Sauté the bananas in the caramel until the fruit has softened and is lightly browned.
4. In a small saucepan, warm the rum.

5   Add the rum to the bananas and
    set it alight with a match. Never
    use a lighter!

For a non-alcoholic dessert

- Once the bananas have been cooked
  remove them from the pan and
  keep warm.
- Add the orange juice to the caramel
  and cook, bubbling, for 10 minutes.
  It will turn into a thick sauce.

---

6   Lay the bananas on the sablés or biscuits
    and spoon the sauce on top.
7   Cut the strawberries into thin slices and
    arrange them with the other berries,
    around the bananas, and garnish with mint
    leaves.
8   Serve with vanilla ice-cream.

Justin's tip: Don't overdo the alcohol. If you
want to get drunk, go to a pub.

him, and down in the changing rooms after a disappointing game against Chumley Court he gave Mee a clip round the ear. This was particularly upsetting to Mee since he was peeing into the mossy urinals at the time, and he sprayed himself and two other squirts from 5B before lashing out in retaliation. Within seconds a mob in various stages of undress had formed a ring around them, baying for blood.

'Fight! Fight! Fight! Fight!' they cried.

'What did you call me?' shouted Mee, confused by this onslaught from his best friend and all-round hero.

'A stinking yob!' came Bathurst's reply, accompanied by a sharp box on the ears that sent Mee tumbling through the crowd and into the showers. That was it. Mee lost all control. But every attack he made was dealt with efficiently, almost effortlessly, by Bathurst's frighteningly accurate blows. He beat Mee back through the changing rooms, smashing him into basins, crunching him into doorframes, narrowly missing clothes hooks and, finally, banging him through the toilet doors and on to the floor, his head in a puddle. Bathurst held him down and allowed himself the smile of the truly sadistic. Only at the last possible moment did Bathurst let him go, leaving Mee to growl his defiance.

'That's it, you've gone too far this time. You can collect your own snotty tuck from now on.' Bathurst's smile as he left indicated that he intended to.

As the crowd dispersed with the universal groan of disappointed rubberneckers, the Scoffers wondered what had been going on. They had only caught a glimpse of the battle, and assumed, quite rightly, that it was nothing to do with them.

Goof, especially, was in a world of his own anyway, imagining the professorial manufacture of alcohol. Adopting the Headmaster's mannerisms, he pointed at a tooth mug.

'Fractional distillation. After 65 degrees Centigrade you have to stop, because then you get alcohol.' He stressed the alcohol, still a bone of some contention for him, 'and alcohol, as you all know, is very bad for you.'

'Not in small doses, it isn't,' reassured Magnus. 'That's why you're in charge, Al. Sukri will get you the pears, and we'll go in tonight.'

Magnus was cut off by a sharp jab from Tava, arrested by the sight of a sodden, bedraggled Mee standing before them. Not sniffing for information as they expected, but holding out his crumpled week's tuck as an offering.

'Pax?'

Tava and Goof were unsure about letting Mee join the Scoffers, but Magnus persuaded them that everybody is entitled to a second chance, including themselves. They couldn't argue with that, but they still didn't like it, and only grudgingly allowed Mee to come on the Poire Williams expedition that night.

As it turned out, Mee proved himself useful when Goof turned out to be less of a chemist than everyone had imagined.

'Nothing's coming out,' pointed out Tava as the Scoffers watched Goof fiddling with the bubbling pipework he had constructed to repeat the Head-master's experiment. Yet Goof remained defiant, checking his thermometers with the authority of a Nobel laureate.

'Of course not. It's only . . . 119 degrees.'

'Watch it, Al,' said Magnus with grave concern. 'We don't want to do a Headmaster.'

Goof's confidence crumpled. 'I think I've done something wrong.'

Nobody knew what to do. None of them had paid attention in class. Except Mee, who was a natural chemist, always had been, ever since he had poisoned his sister's hamster by distilling vinegar into concentrated acid. It was clear to him that Goof had done absolutely everything wrong. He stepped forward and offered his services with his usual diplomacy.

'Here. Let me do it.'

He turned down the roaring Bunsen burner, reconnected the pipework and ran a water supply alongside the apparatus, culminating in the welcome sounds of drip, drip. The test tube started to fill drop by drop with pure pear-juice alcohol.

Mee folded his arms with a certain pride. 'There you go. Poire Mee!'

The Scoffers gave him a small round of applause. Mee had earned his spurs. Clearly Magnus had been right to give him that second chance.

Or had he? Only a few hours later Mee was scampering across the Italianate Gardens, ducking behind the pavilion. There, in the shadows, wearing a long trench coat and hat (despite the clement weather), was Bathurst.

'Did anyone see you?'

'Course not!'

'They're even more stupid than I thought. So what is that pathetic little squirt up to?'

'Digging his own grave, in my opinion.'

Bathurst had not asked for Mee's opinion. Simply the facts. But this was good news, so he overlooked the presumption, and asked to be shown the evidence. A test tube was full of expellable offences for Maggot and his misguided disciples. Maggot was of course the primary target, but the others should go too, if for no other offence than their stupidity. He couldn't believe how easily his plan was working.

Within a few hours, Bathurst was staring into an entire beaker of pear-juice alcohol, which would serve his purposes perfectly. He let out a maniacal laugh, which he had been practising in the mirror. Mee tried to imitate the laugh, but his lack of practice and genuine evil showed. Bathurst slapped Mee on the back, and Mee slapped him back. Not only was this another transgression of the class divide, but he splashed alcohol all over Bathurst's pyjamas.

14

The Big One

With all the excitement of preparing for the Feast at Midnight, Magnus had almost forgotten his fears for his father's life. Until that final letter.

My Dear Boy

I had hoped that by now news from the front might have been somewhat better than it is. Please don't alarm yourself, but I have always treated you as an equal, and I think it only right to keep you fully appraised. I have never, myself, liked surprises. It is always better to fear the worst and hope for the best. That way one is very rarely disappointed.

Magnus dropped the letter at this point, because Charlotte had just prodded him in the back and it fell into the potting wheel, on which Magnus was half-heartedly making a pot.

'Oops, sorry.' She blushed, hoping that Magnus might let her read the letter, and maybe even comment on her nice new pink top.

But he did neither. 'It's OK,' he said quietly.

He fished out the letter from the quick-drying red clay, and slipped it into his potting overalls. Charlotte was not in the mood to be put off, however. Today was her eighteenth birthday, and she hoped against hope that Magnus might have found this out. And maybe he would even organize just a little feast for it.

'Is there going to be another feast soon?'

'I don't think so. They're too dangerous.' Magnus didn't want to talk about feasts right now.

'But you were the one who –' she persisted.

'I know, I know,' he conceded. He had to stop her asking questions, but he didn't want to be rude. So he tried a plausible excuse. 'Chef's got all woossy, and anyway, we're out of tuck.' That should do it, now buzz off.

'I could get some from the village.'

'No . . . We're out of money too.'

'I've got some pocket money –' Clearly she was not going to let this go, and Magnus couldn't bear to keep up the lie a moment longer. He had to resort to the Welsh approach to conversational endings. Brutal and short.

'No! It's just too dangerous!'

Charlotte's world fell apart. Suddenly her birthday was the loneliest day of her whole life. Just as she had got used to the idea of having friends, it was taken away. She very nearly burst into tears right there, on the spot, but her new-found dignity wouldn't allow it. She walked away, through the door, down the corridor, in a daze, hoping that he would call her back, tell her that it was all a mistake.

As soon as she had gone, Magnus pressed on with the letter.

However, one must never be ruled by fear.

Only by risking disappointment can we truly succeed, and only by being surprised do we truly live.

As Magnus listened to Charlotte's receding footsteps he allowed himself a small, sad smile. He would make her eighteenth birthday the best of her whole life. Both for her and for Father, who went on to write:

I fully hope to surprise you yet.

Magnus took a deep breath. If he had allowed himself to dwell on the possibility of losing Father, he would have been unable to go on, but the letter was quite clear. He was to fear for the worst and hope for the best. Otherwise, there was not a damn thing he could do. So letting slip one solitary tear, he read the final paragraph.

And on the subject of surprises, your plan sounds a delight. As Chairman of the Scoffers, I wish you all every success.

Thanks, Dad. Magnus got up from the potting wheel. There was lots to do.

Charlotte, too, was made of sterner stuff than she knew. She was damned if she was going to let her special day run by without acknowledgement from somebody, even if that somebody was her. So she retired to her room, plonked herself down in front of the mirror and decided, yes, to put on that little black dress she'd bought with all her savings at the Top Shop in Dumpton. She'd never dare to wear it in public, of course. The grumpy Saturday assistant at the shop had persuaded her to take the size 8 because, she said grudgingly, Charlotte had the figure to carry it off. Charlotte suspected that they were trying to get rid of that size. All the glamorous local girls with their stilettos and white satin hand-bags had cleaned them out of 12s and 14s. But she hadn't looked too bad when she had been able to find a space in front of the dressing-room mirror. It was probably one of those mirrors that make everybody look thin – convex or concave, Charlotte could never remember which one. Still, there was nobody around to gawp at her now, so, very tentatively, she slipped out of her faded check overall, and held the dress up against her. Go on, she thought, put it on.

She stood there for a moment, her toes pointing awkwardly inwards, tilting her head from side to side. She'd washed her hair, and caked her face in a mud pack she'd found at the Body Shop, and she had to admit that those nasty spots around her chin had definitely gone down. So far so good. What she needed now was some music, so she went over to her old secondhand Grundy music centre and put on her favourite single, 'I Will Always Love You' by Whitney Houston. It was her only single, and she used the repeat function.

She loved Whitney. She closed her eyes and started to sway her hips, dancing out of her pink skirt and blouse, shimmering into that little black dress. And the shop mirror hadn't lied, she looked sort of OK. Her bottom wasn't too big, and she noted for the first time that she had a cleavage. As the song picked up speed, so did she, strutting her stuff up and down the room like Kate Moss on the catwalk, except that she couldn't stop smiling. Out came the hair-dryer and she blew her hair into a big, full wave that swished around her shoulders when she made those dramatic catwalk turns.

The moment of truth. She took off her glasses and the world became a fuzzy place. She liked that. It made everything look soft focus like the heroines do in old movies. Nice black eyeliner gave her eyes, what she could see of them, a certain sophistication; and a hint of blue eye-shadow, just a hint – didn't want to be tarty. Max Factor light cinnamon lip-stick, and a little foundation. Putting her glasses back on for a moment she checked the final result, and was happy with what she saw.

'Well, happy birthday, Charlotte,' she purred in her most confident voice.

The door opened with a bang, and Charlotte's fragile world shattered on impact. Raptor stood aghast at this extraordinary sight of a woman where he'd fully expected to see a girl.

'For heaven's sake, you're not dressed!'

Simply as self-defence, Charlotte lunged for her overall and held it up to her chin, but the new woman was not to be shouted at in this way, certainly not in the privacy of her own home. 'Don't you ever knock?' she said, revealing she was a Longfellow too.

But Raptor had had more practice at this game, and he had the dual advantage of height and volume. 'Don't talk to me in that tone of voice, young lady!'

Charlotte's resolve crumbled and she became a little girl again. 'Sorry, Father.'

'I don't know what's got into you. That little stunt you pulled the other day, bicycling across the cricket pitch. Honestly, it's disrespectful to the school and it's disrespectful to me. Are you deliberately trying to defy me?'

Charlotte started shaking. Her mouth opened, but nothing came out. Raptor didn't wait for the rest. He glowered darkly, let out the sigh of a father who has been driven to his wits' end, and stormed out, leaving Charlotte to turn back to her mirror with red eyes.

Tava's digital watch flashed 9:59; 10:00. Then it beeped. So too did the other three watches on his wrist. Hitting all four buttons with the precision of a boy in tune with all things technological, Tava rolled out of bed, quickly followed by the other Scoffers, which by now meant everybody in the dorm except Bathurst. They assembled around the one Scoffer who wouldn't budge. Goof clenched his eyes shut and snored preposterously loudly.

Magnus gave him a gentle prod. 'Come on, Al, time to go.'

'What?' Goof muttered. 'I'm asleep.'

Tava wasn't going to have any of this nonsense, and reached in to haul him out of bed.

'All right, all right,' shrieked Goof, waving off Tava's forklift, 'I'm coming. Are you sure Raptor's asleep?'

It was a silly question. Nobody could ever be sure of that.

'He definitely won't be if you carry on,' said Tava with searing logic. 'Anyway, who's going to whip the cream if you don't, Al?' This was a much better tack. Goof almost gave way. But Magnus didn't want this to be a press gang. The Scoffers were founded to prevent that kind of thing.

'Nobody has to come if they don't want to,' he whispered. 'But there's going to be a feast tonight, even if it's just me.' It was a brave statement to make. They might have all just decided to slope off back to bed, and he would not have been able to give Charlotte the kind of feast he had in mind.

But, thankfully, Tava's will was firm. 'And me.'

'And me,' joined the others, except Goof.

Who then relented, breaking into a big smile. Forget his dad. 'And me.'

One by one, they crossed the light barrier, treading carefully in each other's footsteps to avoid the creaky floorboards. Mee was in the rear. He stepped into the light and at that moment hit a noisy board. It let out a creak to end all creaks, and, like Magnus all those weeks ago, he froze in the headlamps. Magnus dived out of the safety of darkness to retrieve him, while the others looked in panic at Raptor's door. The silence was unbroken. They were safe – for now. If Magnus hadn't had a lot to think about already, he might have realized that Mee should be watched carefully.

At the end of the corridor, they split up into two prearranged teams. One went down the back stairs towards the chapel and the art room. The other went down the main stairs to the kitchen. Every man knew his task. Like an SAS combat squad, they operated in darkness, without a sound. The Steinway was wheeled out on to the drive and run along planks gathered from the building site down at the stables. Trestle tables were moved from the vestry and were draped in clean white sheets that had been kept aside from last Sunday's laundry.

Ornate 'S' cards, hand-painted by Tava and his art team, marked place settings. Lighted torches with radiator-recharged Duracell batteries were placed face up on the tables, forming a row of candelabra. Dressing-gowns were pinned up to become the appropriate length for smoking jackets, while fresh pillowcases were neatly folded and slung over arms as serving napkins. Pyjama tops were buttoned all the way to the top, and paper ribbons were tied into bow-ties (Burkhart's father had taught him how to do this, so he did everybody's).

In the kitchen, boys from both teams regrouped for the preparation of the chocolate charlotte. Pears and Williams kneaded the biscuit mixture, Tava and Burkhart unwrapped the mounds of tuck and crumbled every ounce of chocolate off every Flake, Dairy Milk and Galaxy into a double boiler that bubbled gooily. Merriman peeled the perfectly ripe little wild orchard pears, leaving long strands of continuous curly skin, while Cubitt sliced the fruit in half, making sure to save the juice. Mee beat egg whites into a flurry of lightness, and then went off to keep cave. Goof, of course, whipped the cream, but with such mastery that not a spot landed any-where except inside the bowl.

And overseeing all of his sous-chefs perform the tasks he had taught them was Magnus, Chef's big white hat falling over his eyes, pointing, praising, licking, tasting and wiping up afterwards.

Finally the chocolate base of the charlotte sat gleaming on the kitchen counter, and, for all Magnus's urging, the eleven boys had conspired to make an unholy mess around them. But none of that mattered when confronted by this most majestic of desserts that awaited its tiny spot of Poire Williams. Mee was called over from the door, and, with a great flourish, he raised his test tube of clear liquid to the light and poured half a teaspoonful into the mix. Then he stepped back, and every Scoffer held his breath at Magnus dipped his little finger into their creation. Father would have been proud. Since that last day they spent together preparing the Poire Belle Hélène when Magnus was sous-chef, how things had changed. Now Magnus was the master of the kitchen, and his sous-chefs waited for his pronouncement on the charlotte.

He dipped the end of his chocolate finger on the tip of his tongue and let the smooth, rich taste settle into his tastebuds. This was the first time he had ever made one of these, but it was as light as one of Father's, and certainly possessed that piquant after-taste delivered by the hint of alcohol. It was exquisite.

Magnus nodded his approval, and the Scoffers let out a collective sigh of relief. This was their finest hour. In no time at all, and after so many weeks of tuck deprivation, they would be standing proudly in front of this lush dessert, poised to reap the rewards. Smiling broadly to each other they followed Magnus in a great huddle as he paraded their creation to the walk-in fridge. It was like a coronation procession in which the charlotte was their crown. All it needed now was forty minutes of cooling. Magnus pulled open the door.

'I knew it! I knew it! I knew it!' shrieked Chef from his hiding place inside the fridge. Judging by the icicles that had formed on his eyebrows, he had been there for some time, and had only survived thanks to multiple layers of furry hats and parkas, and a hot-water bottle strapped to his middle. Pushing back the hanging turbots that had been slapping in his face for hours, Chef sprang out into a most surprised gathering of Scoffers. He leapt forward, they fell back. He kept on going, they kept on falling, tumbling over each other, with Magnus bearing the full brunt of the onslaught, desperately clinging to the charlotte.

'Why are you doing this to me?' screamed Chef. 'Why? Why? Why?'

'We're not –' blurted Magnus, in full retreat.

'You're not what? What? What? What is that?'

'It's a chocolate charlotte,' said Magnus, too shocked to tell anything but the honest truth.

Chef slowed down, narrowing his eyes.

'With pears?'

'Yes.'

'The Scoffier recipe?'

'To the letter.'

Chef now slowed to walking pace. 'Where did you get it?'

'We've just made it. It hasn't set yet. That's why we want to put it in your fridge.'

Chef stopped altogether. His nostrils flared as he hoovered up the rich aromas emanating from the dish. They brought back memories of his childhood when he had been a devoted lover of puddings, but was never allowed them by his rake-thin mother. Oh, the mornings spent loitering outside the bakery in Margate, inhaling those wafts.

'May I?' he asked, out of respect for another chef, presenting his little finger from inside his skiing gloves.

Magnus couldn't be sure whether this was a trap or not, but he was in no position to deny the request. They had been caught red-handed by a close ally of the masters. He was bound to report them: he'd made a public statement about it, he'd suffered arctic conditions to trap them. He meant business, and if he wanted to taste their charlotte, he was welcome. But Magnus could have told him that, after tofu lasagne and fennel pie, he wouldn't approve of it.

'Be our guest,' answered Magnus, his voice quavering.

And then something remarkable happened. Chef visibly wobbled. His whole body rippled with pleasure, and his eyelids closed with delight. 'Mmmm. Mmmmmmmm. Mmmmmmmm. So wonderfully unhealthy.'

Magnus couldn't believe his eyes and ears, but there was PsychoChef, torturer of the gastronomic juices, slayer of tastebuds, surrendering to the dark chocolate side. Mr Health and Fitness had used the words 'wonderful' and 'unhealthy' in the same sentence!

And he went on: 'Put it in the fridge. Now, now, now, now. Forty minutes, at least.'

Mee took the charlotte out of Magnus's hands and laid it down on the bottom tray of the open fridge, being careful to avoid the turbots' tails. Magnus, meanwhile, was forced on the defensive by a newly rejuvenated Chef, whose new sense of personal grievance related to the mess in his kitchen. *In his kitchen!*

All of which gave Mee the perfect opportunity to unleash a whole beakerful of Poire Williams into the charlotte unnoticed, and return to the fold just as Chef was up to speed on his full-scale attack.

'Look at all this mess! Look! Look!'

'We were going to clean up while the charlotte was setting. We always clean up afterwards,' replied Magnus, falling over the other terrified Scoffers.

'You're lying! Lies! Lies! What about the peanut butter?'

Tava and Goof could answer that one. 'That was the Headmaster. We saw him.'

'The Headmaster? I see, the Headmaster!' Chef was incredulous at first, but then it all started to add up. Oh, that old bastard thought he was so clever, bringing in healthy food to please the mothers. It was all for the money. Saved a fortune on meat and desserts, too.

'The Headmaster. Now I see,' mused Chef.

But hold on, he wasn't going to be hoodwinked by these kids! 'And what were you doing in here spying on him?'

'Baking,' said Tava quickly. 'Biscuits? Or was it, the, um . . .'

'Crème caramel. Aux fraises,' added Goof.

Chef had to lean on the counter. It was all too much for him. 'Not with wild strawberries?' he asked, knowing already what the answer would be. He had spotted Oberoi and Tava by the First XI pitch. Chef himself had been waiting for those strawberries to ripen just a day or two more. But then they were gone.

Magnus nodded. Wild strawberries they were. And Chef's heart was now theirs.

They had cleaned every pot and pan to within an inch of its life by the time the charlotte came out of the fridge and received its finishing touches of cream and decorative pears. Chef was genuinely impressed with the industry of these boys. Maybe it was because they reminded him of himself at their age, kept from the foods they wanted to eat by an adult system that made no sense. He had taken back his toque to reassert his authority and rather enjoyed that half-hour, which he knew could never be repeated. For the first time at Dryden he saw the boys as something other than mouths to be fed. He would perhaps consult the boys more in future on the menus, maybe even suggest some room in the curriculum for cookery. Hmm. Something to think about while he gave the counter surfaces his last spot check.

'Not bad,' he said, checking his finger. 'Yes, not bad at all.' This Gove fellow ran a tight ship. And that was a beautiful chocolate charlotte. He felt a welling sense of pride in its creation, which had come, after all, from *his* kitchen. It needed just one finishing touch. He plucked a tiny violet from his lapel and popped it on to the middle of the cake. Dead centre. There. Now it was perfect.

'Now go. Go. Go. Go.' He shooed them off with mock gruffness. 'Go and be naughty elsewhere, you little, little . . . Chefs.'

15

Charlotte's Birthday

Off they fled, down the darkened corridors. Magnus sent eight of the Scoffers out through the Italianate Gardens, while Oberoi and Cubitt were directed up the back stairs to Miss Charlotte's room, where they found her wrapped in her faded overall, fast asleep at her dressing table, Whitney Houston still belting out her love song through an increasingly blunted stylus. The boys fell upon her, pulling her out of that deep slumber that is a pre-bedtime nap.

'Miss Charlotte! Miss Charlotte!' they urged in hoarse whispers.

'What? What is it?' Charlotte was still half asleep, fumbling around for her glasses.

'Come quickly. There's been an accident at the pool.'

'At the pool? At this time of night?'

The boys ignored it. They took an arm each and started lifting her up.

'I'd better get Miss Plunder –'

'There's no time. Please come now!'

How could she resist such a call? Her nature wouldn't allow it. So without telling Miss Plunder, and without taking her glasses, she tripped down the back stairs, across the Italianate Gardens towards the pool house, pulled along by two very determined little boys. From a distance, she looked like a recalcitrant lady walking two very energetic large dogs.

However, they didn't stick around for long. As soon as they had dragged her to the water's edge they let go and vanished into the shadows. Charlotte was left completely alone, unable to see, and able only to hear the quiet lapping of water inches away from her toes. This wasn't funny.

'Look, this is silly. I can't see anything.' Her voice echoed around the high stone-and-glass walls that had been a conservatory addition in the nineteenth century. Oh God, she thought, they're making fun of me again. She must look pretty silly standing there in the darkness. Maybe they were intending to push her into the water? Or worse? She began to get rather frightened.

'Hello? Who's there?' she called out, adopting her bravest tone. No answer. Damn, she hated boys sometimes.

Somewhere in the distance, a church bell announced the arrival of midnight.

Just as Charlotte's mood hit its darkest moment, a single, perfect note floated up through the air. It came from a piano. A piano? In the swimming pool? She must be dreaming. She was sure of it, until the voices began. A harmony, of sorts, singing with great gusto from the darkness behind her.

'Happy Birthday to you, Happy Birthday to you, Happy Birthday, dear Charlotte . . .'

And then the blackness around her drew back to reveal eleven boys in a crescent, each wearing a bow-tie, a smoking jacket and holding a candle.

Yoshi's Cointreau Soufflé (serves 4)

unsalted butter
caster sugar
For the pastry cream:
250 ml milk
½ vanilla pod
3 egg yolks
50g caster sugar
15g plain flour
10g cornflour

For the meringue:
2 egg yolks
2 tbsps Cointreau
8 egg whites
40g caster sugar

1 Butter the insides of 4 small
   soufflé dishes or ramekins. Coat
   with a layer of sugar, tapping out
   any excess.

For the pastry cream:

2 Bring the milk to a boil in a heavy
   saucepan, add the vanilla and simmer gently
   for 10 minutes. Take the saucepan off the
   heat and remove the vanilla pod.

3 Whisk together the egg yolks and sugar,
   then slowly add the flour and cornflour,
   still whisking.

4 Blend half the milk into the egg mixture
   and whisk until smooth. Add the rest of the
   milk and boil for 1 minute. Take off the heat

and transfer this pastry cream to a bowl.

5 Mix it together with 2 egg yolks and the Cointreau.

For the meringue:

6 Preheat the oven to 190°C.

7 Beat the egg whites with a whisk, adding the sugar in two halves. The meringue must be stiff enough so that you can turn some upside-down from a spoon without it falling off. (Do not use an electric whisk as it will create air bubbles that are too fine.)

8 Using a metal spoon, stir 1 spoonful of meringue into the pastry cream.

9 Fold in the rest of the meringue briskly.

10 Divide the mixture between the soufflé dishes. Push the edges of the mixture away from the sides of the dish. (Your little finger is best for this task.)

Bake for about 15 minutes until the mixture has risen and is golden.

Yoshi's tip: Make sure the egg whites are stiff and that the oven is really hot before baking. Soufflés are not difficult. Do not be frightened to try.

'. . . Happy Birthday to you!'

There they stood, a choir of young gentlemen paying tribute to her birthday. As they raised three cheers for her, Magnus stepped forward and offered her his arm. She couldn't believe the joy she felt inside, and attempting to remain as graceful as possible, she took his arm, and let herself be led down an aisle of clapping boys, their beaming faces flickering in the candlelight. If she was already moved, she hadn't seen anything yet, because there, springing to life, was a host of torches that shot their beams upwards into the rafters, illuminating balloons, jugs of orange squash, streamers with her name on them, and the *pièce de résistance*, the chocolate charlotte.

The boys gathered around the piano, on which Goof had just played his first public performance. Magnus offered to take Charlotte's overall. She let it slip into his hands, and revealed her shimmering little black dress underneath. The boys gave her a gasp of approval that made her glad she'd put the dress on earlier, and she granted them a little twirl. Her confidence levels rose with each admiring face. Then somebody shouted, 'Pwang!'

It was Mee. But the others turned on him, defending their fair maiden from such vulgarity, and Goof struck up a blues number on the piano. Charlotte's birthday party had begun in earnest.

It was a most un-English affair. Thanks to the somewhat alcoholic presence in a certain cake, which had been half devoured in under an hour, they all fell away from the delicious food and orange

196

squash to concentrate on the important business of getting down. And did they get down! Strewn with streamers, faces smeared with chocolate, they whirled like dervishes and shook tail feathers like Tasmanian devils. Charlotte was centre stage, tossed in mock Scottish reel from boy to boy, shrieking with laughter and glowing with the radiance of the truly loved. The only two not hurling themselves fully into the event were Mee, holding himself back unnoticed from the fray, and Magnus, who simply sat at the piano, wanting to remember every second of this event.

Charlotte bounded up to him, and over Goof's crashing ivories she shouted into Magnus's ear: 'Thank you, Magnus! This is the best birthday I've ever had. I feel really woozy!'

Magnus was suddenly shy. He hadn't done all this for her thanks, and certainly not for the big, pouting kiss she planted on his forehead. Wow! He would never forget that unrestrained expression of emotion, ever. But right now there were other distractions, such as Tava, stuffing another slice of charlotte into his mouth, and then swaying slightly, staggering backwards towards the pool's edge. His curly-toed slippers wobbled, his arms started making helicopter movements, his eyes bulged, and then he was in.

Splash!

This feast was supposed to be poolside dining, not in-pool swimming. Magnus started to push his way through the party to pull Tava out.

Splash! Goof was in, too. Then every boy hurtled

towards the pool, gesticulating wildly as Tava let out a great shoot of water, like a blue whale in the deep ocean. Cubitt found it so funny he left his back unguarded and Oberoi took the opportunity to topple him in. Like lemmings, the rest followed the great rush for the water, taking Magnus and Charlotte with them. Magnus realized that getting out would bring the party to an end, and he didn't want that. He didn't want anything to spoil this evening for Charlotte.

Only Mee remained dry, lurking by the trophy cabinets that saluted Dryden's pre-eminence as England's top swimming school. He peered out through the windows that held in the noise of the festivities, wondering how long Bathurst would be. Then he saw the signal. The floodlights outside the pool house flashed on, off, on, off. Unnoticed by those inside but not by those sleeping in the main building. Bathurst had found the power switch and was sending out his message. This time, he would spoil their fun – as long as Raptor had left his curtains open sufficiently to let the floods hit his face.

He had. As he lay in his sepulchral bed, hands folded over his chest like an entombed medieval knight (or a prince of darkness in his coffin) his closed eyes were blasted with a flash of light, then darkness, then another blast. In a blink his head was up and alert, his face pressed against the window. The contravention of Dryden rules became all too evident. From the bushes Bathurst saw that his work was done and he slunk back to the dorm just as Raptor in flowing piped dressing-gown catapulted across the Italianate Gardens.

'Cave, Raptor!' was the first anyone heard above the splashing. Goof had been taking a breather on the lowest of the three high-diving boards, draping himself across it like a movie star, when he spotted that familiar tank division rolling relentlessly in their direction. And suddenly, even in his rather wobbly state, the whole world was thrown into sharp focus. Well, sharpish. He tried to get up and run back along the board, but his steering was all wonky and he found himself in the water again, just as everybody else was flailing about in an attempt to get out. It was chaos. Dressing-gowns billowed over their heads, and a mass of slippers had to be gathered in the great escape. There was more panic than if someone had shouted 'Shark!'

Only Charlotte and Magnus kept their heads, pushing and pulling the others out of the water and propelling them off to the changing rooms and the emergency fire exit. By the time Raptor burst through the front doors, Charlotte was shielding the getaway of Magnus and a very much worse for wear Tava. Raptor never saw them. He was utterly transfixed by the débris that littered the hallowed territory of his second-favourite sporting institution, the swimming hall. And the first, and only, person he could actually make out in the gloom was Charlotte, in a clinging wet black dress. His rising fury took only a split second to hit the top.

'*What . . . on earth . . . is going on?*' he roared.

Amazingly, Charlotte did not retreat from the blast. Instead she tripped unsteadily towards him, saying nothing.

'What are you doing here? You know you are not allowed to be here. Charlotte! Come here! Charlotte!'

She turned on her heel and walked away, swaying her hips and tossing a defiant look over her shoulder.

'Charlotte!' He couldn't believe his eyes. 'What are you playing at?'

She stopped suddenly, and this action, for the first time ever, stopped him.

'What does it look like? I'm having a swim. A very nice swim, in fact.' She spat out the words.

Raptor did not appreciate her tone, but now was not the time to argue over delivery. He wanted facts. 'You know the pool is out of bounds –'

'I am not one of your pupils!'

Good Lord, she had quite a voice on her. He'd never noticed. She didn't sound like her mother at all.

'Come to think of it, I'm not even a boy.' From where he was standing, that much was clear. And there was that tone again. Raptor actually found himself backing up a few steps. She looked as if she had more ammo, and wasn't afraid to use it. 'By the way, did you know it was my birthday today?'

She got him on that one, but he wasn't about to admit it. 'Ah, umm, yes. Yes, of course I did.'

'So I thought I'd have a party. Isn't that what you're supposed to do for your birthday? Bit of music, lovely cake. Here, try some.' With a violent thrust, she rammed some leftover charlotte into his chest, forcing him to catch it.

He stared at the cake, then at the piano and the surrounding wreckage. It really was an appalling mess, the whole situation, and clearly shouting at Charlotte was not doing the trick. He would have to take another tack. Get to the root of the problem. Somebody had engineered all of this. An act of defiance. The open flouting of school rules. Only one person had the independence of spirit to do that.

'Gove's behind all this, isn't he? That boy is a terrible influence on the school.'

What followed scared even Raptor. Charlotte reached over to the trophy cabinets and swiped every last priceless cup into the pool or on to the concrete edge. The noise was deafening. That was absolutely his limit.

'Be careful! Those things are priceless!' He charged at her, but in a flash she was scaling the cabinet shelves and leaping out of reach on to the ladder to the diving boards. Up she went, unsteadily now, her wet feet slipping on the smooth metal rungs, until she hoisted herself on to the top board, thirty feet up.

'For God's sake! Just listen to yourself!' she screamed, rattling the thin railing that stood between her and a drop on to the concrete below. 'Why has everything got to be so simple for you? You and your stupid rules. And your stupid system. You've got to be good at cricket, good at Latin, good for the school. Or you're not worth talking to!'

'That's not true, Charlotte —' countered Raptor.

'Yes, it bloody well is! And I've had enough. I've had *enough*!' She teetered on the platform. Raptor's heart stopped and he lunged forward.

'For goodness sake, be careful!'

Charlotte's foot swung back on to the platform, missed and she fell. It was only a desperate clutch at the railing that saved her. She dragged herself back up.

'It's a bit late to start caring now,' she said, this time in a quiet, sad voice that told the story of eighteen years.

A tinge of regret jabbed under Raptor's skin, and worked its way towards his heart. He wanted to say something. Something comforting. But there was no time. Charlotte ran forward, and sprang into the air. Like a great, beautiful bird she arched her body and released her arms in a declaration of freedom, hitting the water with barely a ripple. With an underwater glide she was at the shallow end, then out and through the front doors, without so much as a backward glance. It was a magnificent exit.

Raptor was left, quite literally, holding the cake, calling feebly after her, his voice broken by the weight of his crime and the severity of her judgement.

For the first time in his seventy-three years, Raptor just didn't know what to do. There were simply too many offences for him to decide on a suitable course of action. The blatant disregard for the rules. The cheek. Finding the culprits would be easy enough, but then what? The boys, whoever they were, hadn't just been out of bounds (200 lines) and after lights out (100 lines). They had moved the piano (two hours' gardening), stolen from the linen cupboard (500 lines), lit candles (rustication), got hold of food (200 lines), and even roped in Charlotte. What was the punishment for turning his daughter against him? As he made his way wearily up the stairs, Raptor felt very old. If that Gove really was to blame, the chances were that most of 3A was involved. 3A, the fast stream. 3A that thrived on academic excellence and performance on the sports field. V. E. Longfellow, 3A and excellence had all been synonymous for close to forty years. But with this new development, the whole of 3A would most likely be – expelled?

Raptor shuddered at the thought, and stood dead still in the silent corridor of the west wing. Then his senses picked up something. He couldn't put his finger on it, but there was definitely something wrong with the picture. There was a sweet smell. Coming from where? He was outside Miss Plunder's room, and he sniffed around. But it wasn't coming from inside, it was the cake, or what was left of it. He raised the platter right up to his face. Raptor had kept the remains of the charlotte as evidence, but it wasn't until now that he worked it out. It was unmistakable. Alcohol, and lots of it. Expulsion was now a definite.

Before he had time to reflect fully on the implications, his thoughts were interrupted by a door swinging open, almost hitting him.

'Oh, Major Longfellow. You're still up.' It was

Miss Plunder, dressed for bed. She looked at the charlotte. 'Is that for me?'

'Oh no, it's evidence, I'm afraid,' stammered Raptor. 'The boys have been up to no good.'

'I see,' she replied in an understanding tone. 'I have just put the kettle on. Why don't you come in and tell me all about it?'

'Oh no, I couldn't. Shouldn't . . .' But then Raptor paused. Why not? 'Well, maybe just a quick one.'

Miss Plunder's big round face broke out into a smile. As she moved aside to usher Raptor in, she added with a wink, 'Why don't you bring that in, and we can keep an eye on it?'

With no further ado, the two of them disappeared into her boudoir.

Over in Small Boys, the scene was rather more chaotic. Pillows, duvets, teddy bears, arms and legs were everywhere. The dormitory was more like a squat that night, with eleven boys trying to sleep off the effects of the most almighty rave Dryden had ever seen. Drunken snores echoed around the room.

In the far corner, Bathurst was still awake. He surveyed his domain with some satisfaction. He had successfully pulled off his most elaborate plan to date. Gove would be out, he would be back in, and all would be back to normal. Tuck tariffs would be resumed as before, and he would be able to report business as usual to his dad. All in all, a not unsatisfactory outcome for him, for his family and, of course, for Dryden. Bathurst closed his eyes and fell into the deepest, most relaxing sleep he had had since the beginning of term.

And so it was only the nightingales and the owls that heard the last bit of human activity that night, coming from the west wing of the Palladian mansion. '*Oooh!* Major Longfellow!'

'I have some very bad news to report this morning,' boomed the Headmaster to the assembled crowd. The chapel service had come to an end, with most of the school enthusiastically belting out 'Dear Lord and Father of Mankind'. But the 3A pew was unusually quiet, and with good reason. Eleven of them were nursing the mother of all hangovers for the first time in their lives. Breakfast had been rather strained, and it had been a struggle for them to keep down their bran muesli.

'To cut a long story very short, there have been boys at the pool after lights out. Eating.' The Headmaster looked around, trying to spot the guilty parties. The crowd shifted uncomfortably, murmuring. 3A remained as inscrutable as they could, trying not to retch and shielding their eyes from the bright sunlight.

'We can resolve this very quickly. You know who you are. All those responsible, can we have a show of hands, please?' A polite enough request, which, not surprisingly, met with an equally well-mannered silence. Not a single hand went up. The Headmaster waited a little bit longer, but still nothing.

'I see,' he said finally. 'Well, we can do this the

hard way, if you wish. We will wait. We will wait as long as we have to.'

Magnus looked around at his bleary-eyed cohorts. A plan started to form. He had seen it happen in films a lot: one person took the fall for all of them. But before he could say anything, Tava read his mind. 'Don't do anything,' he whispered through clenched teeth. 'They don't know anything.'

'It won't be that serious,' the brave leader replied. After all, what could he get? Five hundred lines, max. But Tava was holding down Magnus's arm.

'Right the way through half term, if need be,' the Headmaster continued. It was a threat. Groans went up from all parts of the room. And that clinched it for Magnus. It had been his idea, and if anybody was responsible, it was him. Tava was now actually sitting on Magnus's left hand. So Magnus raised his right.

The Headmaster allowed himself a thin smile. He hadn't become Headmaster for nothing. He knew all too well what really hurt. Works every time. 'There's one. Now what about the others?'

'There were no others, sir. It was just me.'

'I find that rather difficult to believe,' said the Headmaster with an amused look, 'since there was a grand piano involved.'

Fair point. Very slowly, the Scoffers all owned up, straining at the effort to raise their arms and keep them raised through their stupor. Mee was trying to look small and unnoticeable, but Oberoi forced him to join in. Bathurst just shrugged. *C'est la vie.*

The Headmaster was finally satisfied. 'That's more like it. See me in my study now, please.'

Before they knew it, the eleven Scoffers were lined up in front of the Headmaster's big desk, heads bowed. Both the Headmaster and Raptor stood looking at them, but, curiously, Raptor seemed distracted. The room was a lot less friendly than Magnus remembered it, and there wasn't an éclair in sight. Not that he wanted one: the mere thought of food brought on waves of nausea. When the Headmaster broke the silence, eleven stomachs had to add knotting to their already delicate states.

'This is very much more serious than I had originally thought,' he began, picking up the platter on which the tiniest sliver of the charlotte now sat. 'Major Longfellow hardly needed to tell me that this cake has been laced with an enormous quantity of alcohol.' He was right; even from the very small piece that remained, the whiff of Poire Williams was pervading the room. 'Supplying alcohol to minors is not only against the rules of Dryden, it is against the law of the land.'

'It was only half a teaspoon, sir,' pleaded Magnus. Honesty was the best approach.

'Be quiet, Gove, you're in enough trouble already. Lying will only make matters worse.'

'I'm not lying –'

'*Will you be quiet!*' With veins throbbing on his forehead, the Headmaster steamed on: 'You deserve to be expelled, every last one of you!' He rarely raised his voice, but these boys' actions merited it. He had never, ever, been so incensed.

'Umm. Headmaster . . .' injected Raptor quietly, passing over a note he had just scrawled. The Headmaster was brought to a sudden halt, his mouth half open in preparation for the next part of his tirade. He couldn't believe it! He was being interrupted! Still, the Headmaster put on his glasses and took a look. Suddenly, the world seemed a very different place, even though there wasn't much on the note, just: '£9,000 × 11 = £99,000 p.a.'

'Yes . . . Thank you,' replied the Headmaster as casually as he could. Raptor, of course, was right. Many a business has folded as a result of a single rash decision. The Headmaster sat down and changed into super-avuncular mode. 'However. Midnight feasts are one thing, used to have them myself in the past. On this occasion I'm going to allow Major Longfellow to deal with you in his own fashion. For now you may go.' He thought he had saved that one rather well.

As for the Scoffers, somehow even the threat of Raptor dealing with them wasn't as frightening as the wrath that the Headmaster had just shown himself capable of. They began to file out of the room silently, knowing that the school would be eager to hear what had happened. It was time for 3A to prepare for its fifteen minutes in the limelight. Magnus still felt guilty for getting everyone into trouble, but they had had the best party of all time, hadn't they? But there were questions, still. What would happen to the Scoffers as an institution? Could they carry on? Who had alerted Raptor to the swimming pool? And how could half a teaspoon of alcohol have been so potent?

Before Magnus could begin to answer any of these mysteries, he was stopped in his tracks.

'Gove, you will stay behind.' The Headmaster was back to his authoritative self.

16
Times Change

The 3A form room was bustling with its usual level of activity. Bathurst and Mee had taken up their positions as keepers of the gate and collectors of tuck, and at that moment Mee was grappling with Goof's fast-diminishing Maltesers. The others, who had already paid their price of admission, were pretending nothing was amiss. All told, it was just another day at Dryden Park.

Then they fell silent, and looked to the doorway. There was Magnus, in his jeans and Converse All-Stars, dragging his heavy trunk. The more recently initiated Scoffers looked away, denying that anything was wrong. But Tava and Goof, those two stalwart allies, were not so sure. Yes, they did have 400 lines and two hours of gardening to do by the weekend, but my God had they had fun earning them. Being part of the Scoffers was worth a thousand lines.

Bathurst was more brutal. 'You know something, Maggot? Nobody ever really liked you here. Bye-bye.' And with a limp wave he dismissed Magnus and went back to his tuck mountain. Mission accomplished.

The Headmaster had hesitated at expulsion, but the consequences of not taking firm action had been too great to contemplate. Getting rid of the whole of 3A would definitely have bankrupted Dryden. Expelling Gove as the leader had been the perfect compromise solution. Business was all about compromises. Magnus was told to pack his things and be out of the school by Sunday lunchtime.

And now it was Sunday, and it was nearly time for liver and cabbage. As Magnus struggled through the trophy corridor for the last time, he thought back to his first day, when he had seen all those photos and trophies for the first time. A lot had happened in the five short weeks. There was still no framed memento of a cooking club, or indeed of the Scoffers. Nevertheless Magnus had shared his passion with his friends, and he was happy about that.

But he now had to leave behind these friends. He would write to them, and send them recipes, but Magnus had no idea when he might see them again.

Suddenly Magnus turned around, and there they were: Tava and Goof, lifting up the heavy end of the trunk. And, quite unlike that first day when they had only helped under strict instructions from the Headmaster, here were two chaps helping a mate. Because they wanted to. They didn't care about Bathurst's sniggering. If their best friend was leaving, they were going to see him off.

The Scoffers dropped the heavy trunk on to the gravel of the driveway, and plonked themselves down on it. It was an awkward moment. Nobody knew what to say.

'I still don't get it,' Tava began.

'Nor do I,' answered Magnus resignedly.

'It was only five ccs of alcohol and –' Goof had gone back to his pre-Scoffers nervousness, and was waving his hands about wildly.

'Mee's the only one who knows anything about it, but it doesn't matter now.' Before Magnus could say any more, the bells cut him off.

'It's lunch.'

'Liver and cabbage.'

Magnus got up and tried to look cheerful. 'You'd better go now. Bye, Sukri. Bye, Al.'

'Bye, Magnus.'

'Bye, Magnus.'

Because this was England, there was no hugging. Because they were boys, there was no kissing. And because this was prep school, there was no shaking of hands. But they were Scoffers. So as they stood there, under the magnificent stone portico, they rubbed their tummies in the Scoffers' salute. Without another word, Tava and Goof headed off to the delights of the dining hall, and Magnus was alone again. He sat himself down and gazed into the distance. The mile-long drive was still a mile long, and through the misty haze, he could just make out the obelisk at the far end, commemorating the brave but pointless deaths of eight hundred men back in the eighteenth century. A significant historical event certainly, but for now the uncertainty of his immediate fate was a much greater worry for Magnus. He sighed, and resolved just to wait, as the Headmaster had told him to. But for whom? Or for what?

*

The scene in the dining hall was seemingly quite normal. The boys sat at their usual places and were settling down for a spot of lunch. Bathurst had taken back his pole position next to Raptor and was wolfing down his food with some relish. But, on closer inspection, the mood around the 3A table was quite a lot less jolly. The faces were long, and Raptor was certainly not his usual stern self. Even he had been a little sad to see Gove go, and shared at least some of the boys' melancholy gloom.

'I don't know what you're all whingeing about,' Bathurst stated authoritatively. 'Gove deserved it. Didn't he, Mee?'

But Mee wasn't sure. He wasn't sure at all. It had been fun to start with, being a spy. Taking instructions, clandestine operations, accomplishing the mission and all that; it was just like 007. But having got Magnus actually kicked out, he was having second thoughts. Bathurst had gone too far this time.

'Did he, Mee?' It was Goof, and his tone would have done any grand inquisitor proud.

'Course he did. Don't you agree, sir?' Bathurst was not inviting debate. He was just stating the facts. He looked to his greatest ally for confirmation that he was back in business. But Raptor was lost in his own thoughts, and it was only when the whole table looked to him for a reply that he snapped out of it.

'What? Oh, you're playing Hawtrey's today, aren't you? Well, they'll give you a run for your money, Bathurst.'

That clinched it. Mee was sure that there was

now enough support around the table to put his plan in action. He suddenly got up and scurried out of the room, ignoring Raptor's calls for him to sit down.

Nobody had offered Magnus any lunch, but he wasn't hungry. He just carried on staring at the horizon, hoping that someone, or something, would appear. He felt like T. E. Lawrence looking for Aqaba.

Which was wholly appropriate, since it was just then that in the far distance, through the chilly shimmering haze, appeared a mirage. So faint that Magnus couldn't make out what it was. He screwed up his eyes. One thing was for sure. It was coming his way, slowly getting bigger. As it approached the gate, Magnus stood up. It wasn't Sherif Ali on his proud shining mount, but it wasn't far off: a 1951 $4\frac{1}{2}$ Litre Big Bore Little Boot Mark VI Bentley, with velvet green coachwork, glided majestically into the driveway. Magnus could see that there was a man in a cap sitting in the front driving, but beyond that it was all rather unclear.

The car silently came to a halt beside Magnus. Every inch of its dark-green body was spotless. The driver stared dead ahead, not moving, not saying anything. Then the back door opened. Magnus hadn't noticed anyone in the back, but –

'My dear boy!' said Father, and hugged Magnus with a warmth and affection unprecedented at Dryden Park. Magnus was suddenly no longer the President of the Scoffers, and the leader of men, but a ten-year-old boy basking in the love of his father. Father was immaculate in his casual gear, with a silk cravat that matched his brand-new cardigan, purchased especially for the occasion. He was still a little frail, and his knees were covered by a cashmere travelling rug, but none of these details mattered to Magnus at that moment. Father was alive, he was here, and Magnus was going home with him.

'Have they given you any lunch yet?' asked Father. This was a father that knew his son. Magnus shook his head and was surprised to remember that he was famished. 'Oh!' Father cried, shocked. 'In you get.' Father slid over to the far side with a stifled grunt of pain, and helped Magnus in. Without a word, the chauffeur had the car in gear, and the three of them were driving away. Magnus looked out through the back window. It had only been a few weeks, but it felt like half his life. As they continued down the long drive, the building got smaller and smaller. It was hard for Magnus to imagine that so much had happened in the ever-diminishing dot. But one thing he knew for certain: he was looking at Dryden Park, Preparatory School for Boys aged 7 to 12, for the very last time.

'You know, Magnus . . .' said Father gently. He spoke slowly, leaving long pauses between the words. It was his way of heightening the drama, raising expectations. Magnus was hooked. 'There's an old mill house near here . . . Do an awfully good treacle tart, I remember. Sure they're still there.' Magnus was entranced. Father and food. No other combination could possibly top that. He snuggled up close and relished every detail of Father's plan for them. 'And this evening . . . Oh, I've got something very special in mind for us . . .'

Mee bounded purposefully back into the dining hall, clutching a red-and-white bundle to his chest. He approached the 3A table, took the bundle up to his face, inhaled deeply and then tossed it disgustedly into the salad bowl. Raptor thought that behaviour rather unhygienic, and gave Mee a disapproving look. But Mee could not be intimidated into submission. His eyes were alight with inner fury. He stood there, alternately staring at the bundle and Bathurst. Nobody, including Raptor, knew what this little ritual was meant to signify.

It was Tava who ventured to speak first. 'What is it, Mee?'

Mee didn't answer. He didn't need to. He just kept on staring, burning a hole in Bathurst's skull. Tava reached forward to examine the bundle. Like a striking snake, Bathurst lunged across the table to snatch it away. But Tava got to the bundle first. Bathurst's hand hit the salad bowl and sent it careering into Oberoi's face, hitting him square in the front teeth. Tava gave the bundle a good sniff. Then he too fired an accusing look in Bathurst's direction.

Bathurst wanted to end this game of pass-the-parcel cleanly and quickly. 'Give it here, Tava, you fat bedwetter!'

This form of diplomacy was unlikely to induce

Tava to hand it back with roses attached. Sure enough, as Bathurst lunged at his throat, he passed it on to Oberoi, who sniffed as best he could despite his broken teeth, and passed it on.

Bathurst sprinted round the table, snatching, grabbing and wrestling to get to the bundle, but it eluded him every time. Instead, he hit plates and jugs, smashing them to smithereens.

'Cubitt! Pears! Williams! Merriman! Burkhart! Green Minor!' barked Raptor from the end of the table, as he followed the bundle's progress. 'Green Minor! Give it to me!' But Goof couldn't hand over anything. He was in a head lock, having the bundle prised from his hands by Bathurst, now demonic with lack of control. His eyes bulged and he would gladly have killed Goof had it not been for the interference of an even stronger force.

'*Bathurst!!*' roared Raptor, grabbing the bundle himself, and pulling Bathurst away from a half-strangled Goof. 'Sit down!'

'But, sir –'

'*Sit down!*'

Bathurst was trapped. The bundle was in the hands of the one person out of whom he could not kick the living daylights. He had better calm down, play the innocent, make out it was all a little schoolboy prank. He sat down and tried to resume his superior air. But he watched, very closely, what Raptor did next.

Raptor unfolded the red-and-white bundle to reveal that it was a pyjama top, somewhat damp. He raised it to his face to check the nametape and sure enough, emblazoned by good old Mr Cash, was that familiar name that had always caused him such a flush of pride: BATHURST, R. R.

Raptor's eyebrows furrowed. He was not with the plot quite yet. But then he detected an odour he'd smelt somewhere before. A whiff of alcohol. Raptor's beak lowered itself gently into the material and he inhaled deeply into those cavernous lungs. The smell was unmistakable. It was identical to the cake, and not just one spot but a whole visible stain across the front of the pyjamas. Two dark eyes swivelled in their sockets and rested on their target: Bathurst, R. R.

The target gulped, and issued an uneasy smile. 'Please, sir . . . Oh, sir, it was just a joke . . .'

But, funnily enough, Raptor was not laughing. First Charlotte had walked out on him, then Miss Plunder had walked in on him. Then his least favourite, Gove, had been expelled, wrongly, while his very favourite, Bathurst, had been acclaimed, wrongly again. He had nothing to say to Bathurst or 3A. Nothing to teach them. He needed a period of quiet, to think and to reassess.

'Sir . . .'

'Bathurst. Be quiet,' Raptor commanded in a whisper. And he was scarier in those few quiet words than he had ever been at full volume. Bathurst said nothing more. The eyes of the whole dining hall were now upon him, shouting their silent condemnation. Surely not the whole school was against him now? He looked to Mee for support. But Mee was busy lifting cottage cheese on to his fork. Then, suddenly, he tossed it straight into

Bathurst's right eye. Bathurst shook his head in disbelief, only to have his left eye filled with a greenish and rather hard tomato. Goof had spoken. Shards of lettuce flew from Tava's hand and filled Bathurst's hair.

Raptor was still too stunned to speak or move. The whole room erupted with the cry of 'Food Fight!' and liver, cabbage and non-calorific salad items came raining down from all directions. Only at that point, miraculously untouched by enemy fire, did he throw down his napkin and make his way to the exit. Casting one look back at everything he had ever cared about in such chaos, he stepped out into the bright sunlit day and considered play-ing a gentle game of croquet.

He walked away from an unforgettable scene. For the boys and for Dryden, things would never be the same again. For Monsieur Jourdren, his mauve suit would never recover from the onslaught of so many clashing beetroots. The Chaplain, too: his eyesight would never again be what it had been after his glasses smashed under the weight of a stale wholewheat roll's direct hit. As for Bathurst: well, he got what he deserved. But he never changed. Even in one's wildest dreams of how the world should be, people like Bathurst will always continue to exploit whoever gets in their way. It is the rest of us, with neither the arrogance of Bathurst nor the resolve of Magnus, who change in their presence.

17
Vale

In spite or perhaps as a result of all the recent upheavals, there was a cheerful, almost jolly atmosphere in the air as Dryden gathered for its Monday assembly. The morning light was brighter than ever, suggesting that spring had finally, in mid-June, come to Dumpton. The Chaplain brought the service to an end with a most hearty 'Amen', which was repeated enthusiastically by the congregation. The Headmaster took up his position at the lectern, his face a picture of sunniness, his most colourful bow-tie adding to the brightness of the room.

'Now I have a number of farewells to be said this morning,' he boomed in his usual oratorical manner. 'First off, Magnus Gove of 3A, who left the school yesterday, is looking forward to a stint at the Scoffier School in Paris. And our under-matron, Miss Charlotte, has left us for more exotic climes. Lucky her.'

Exotic was not the word Charlotte would have used for the climate she was now in. It was coming down by the bucketload, drenching her in her flimsy anorak, soaking through her two cardigans and right the way to the bone. All around her, in the sheep-dotted moonscape, the rain was turning rivulets into rivers that rushed along the road around her ankles. But her spirits were high because, as everybody knows, the first faltering steps towards freedom are painful ones. She had her new Ray-Bans and a hand-made, flowery sign that said all it needed to say: ABROAD PLEASE.

She had stood on this road for some hours now, not knowing that it was the very same spot where Magnus had waited for his lift to Paris. She was tired and she felt a cold coming on.

'Aaaaa-tishoo!' She dipped her hand into her pocket to pull out a damp tissue and found something quite different. A soggy but untouched envelope addressed to her. She gasped audibly as she recognized the confident handwriting of her father. She was immediately filled with trepidation. She spun around, scouring the hills, as if he might appear from behind a rock and wrap another cage around her. He must have slipped the note into her anorak that night after their little 'discussion' in the pool. How typical of him to have had the last word. She was angry but brave enough now to take his criticism.

She peeled off the dark glasses, reverting to her reading specs, and opened the envelope. Inside was a birthday card. It wasn't very pretty, and the poem on the front was really cheesy, but this was the first time he had sent her a birthday card. And inside was a fistful of £20 notes and a letter from him:

My Dear Girl,
    A little something to help you on your way.
With love from
    Dad

Tears rushed up and she let out great heaving sobs. She wasn't sure what she was crying about. It was a mixture of everything, and when she'd finished she felt truly free.

Somebody up there must have noticed, because at that very moment a classic Bentley hummed round the corner and pulled up beside her. Naturally, Magnus and his father were happy to have her along for the ride, all the way to Paris. Magnus suggested that she might stay for a few days and take Father for reviving walks. Fate, Charlotte thought, was truly smiling at her. And she would never know that Magnus had asked Father's driver to take every small road in the surrounding countryside until they found her.

Meanwhile, the Headmaster was soldiering on. 'And last, but by no means least, I'm sure you'll all join me in bidding farewell to Major Longfellow and to Miss Plunder, who are leaving us after many years of dedicated service to the school. They will be sorely missed.'

There were murmurs of surprise around the room, but neither Raptor nor Miss Plunder was giving anything away. Then: 'And congratulations are in order, on their forthcoming marriage.' Massive intakes of breath all round, and the happy couple looked up for the first time and smiled.

A solitary 'Pwang' rose up. In amongst the organized cheering, more scattered 'Pwangs' could be heard, which slowly built into a chorus, gaining in numbers, and therefore in confidence. Only one person remained silent. His name was Bathurst. Setting up Gove, said the Headmaster, was a cowardly and expellable offence, but he would keep the young Bathurst in the school, albeit stripped of his scholarship, in return for a generous contribution to the sports hall and some timely tips on 'safe' Lloyd's syndicates from Black Jack himself. Bathurst did not want to go home for half term.

Raptor and Miss Plunder responded to the cheers with happy bows. Then the Headmaster put up his hand to quieten the room.

'That's quite enough of that, thank you. Major and Mrs Longfellow will be going on to Hawtrey's School, where Major Longfellow will be taking up the headmastership. And, finally, Monsieur Jourdren has asked me to let you know that until the rodent exterminators give us the all-clear, wind band practices will take place in the gym.'

Things would never change at Dryden Park.

* * *

'*Au revoir*, Magnus,' Monsieur Vaudron said quietly. He hugged Magnus warmly, and kissed him on both cheeks.

Magnus returned his embrace warmly. As Vaudron's heavy footsteps pounded down the stairs, Magnus pushed the oak door shut. Vaudron was always the last to leave. He and Father had passed many a night arguing into the early hours with a bottle of armagnac about the merits of sabayon over crème pâtissière, or white chocolate over dark. Now even he was gone.

Magnus looked around. Marie-Claire would be back in the morning to clear up. It was time for Magnus to sit down with just the family. Not that Mother was there. Magnus hadn't seen her in over four years, and no one knew where she was to tell her of her husband's death. But Magnus wasn't sad about her absence, because the people he cared about were with him that night.

Tava and Goof had changed little in nine years. After Clifton College, Goof had embarked on a trip around Europe with his Interrail card, and had couchetted over from Dresden as soon as he had heard the news. Gone were the glasses, to be replaced by contact lenses, but he was still thin as a pencil, white as a sheet and fashion was clearly not one of his interests. Similarly, Tava was his usual round self, although it was well hidden under an Armani suit, and he sported a rich tan. He had left Harrow a year early to join his father's business, and it was only because of the start of Ramadan two days before that he had been able to break away from negotiations in Riyadh and First Class it to Paris.

'I'm starving,' said Magnus, rubbing his stomach. He suddenly realized that all he had had that day was a single marquise.

'There's no more food left.'

'And it's raining outside.'

Magnus laughed. Nothing had really changed. 'Come on, the walk will be good for us. There's a place just on the other side of the river.'

They braved the warm spring shower and ran through the empty cobbled streets. And there it was, tucked in between an agence de voyages and a pharmacie: a tiny little restaurant no wider than the car parked in front of it was long, bursting with activity. Two waiters were just folding up the umbrellas and taking the pavement tables out of the rain.

As soon as they saw the sign in the window, the three men made the Scoffers' salute, and, crossing the road, ducked into the inviting comfort of Brasserie Charlotte.